JUST ONE *Love*

Author of the Kiss Me Crazy Series

JAMI ROGERS

Just One Love

Copyright © 2018 by Jami Rogers

Editor: Julie Sturgeon, CEOEditor, ceoeditor.com

Copyediting/Proofreading: Casey Dawes, Concierge Self-Publishing, www.ConciergeSelfPublishing.com

Visit my website: www.authorjamirogers.com

❀ Created with Vellum

JUST ONE *Love*

JAMI ROGERS

JUST ONE LOVE

THE BLACK ALCOVE SERIES BOOK 6

JAMI ROGERS

CHAPTER ONE

Abby

Slashing someone's tires doesn't make you crazy, does it? Maybe a little.

What if they deserve it? I mean, let's say your boyfriend cheated on you with another woman. That might not be reason enough, but what if, just last night, he told you he loved you? Ding, ding, ding, we have a motive!

All I've wanted in life is to fall in love. True, deep, passionate, real love. The love you only see in movies or read about in books. I want a man who is going to pick me first. A guy who smiles when the first thing he sees is me as he wakes up, and recognizes how lucky he is to be with me. Someone who thinks about me all day, who can't wait to see me the moment he comes home. Someone who makes me happy, who I can trust, and who won't take advantage of me when I give him the same. The list of what I want is long, and right now, in my life, this man doesn't exist. He never has, and I'm not sure he ever will.

Instead, I'm stuck with reality. Hence slashing tires.

"Remind me again why I'm here?" Beth pulls her green Nitro to a stop along the curb.

I glance over to the one friend who has been there for me through all my bad decisions in the last few years. And there are a lot. She deserves a prize or something. Her loyalty to me has been the best, and it's the exact reason she is here right now. I needed someone I could trust to come with me.

The stars provide the minimal glow that I need, and, thankfully, the wind is calm, offering the picture-perfect summer night. The street lamps are dim, and because it's getting late, the houses that line the street all look to be closed down for the evening, with porch lights the only signs someone is home. Everything would be perfect if it weren't for one house. The one I specifically need to not have every single light on.

"I need support," I tell her.

The light from the windows helps display the perfectly manicured lawn and the flowerbeds that sit under the two front windows on each side of the front door. I don't remember their names, but the flowers looks like the hair off the toy trolls. *I should dig them up and take them home with me.*

"Abby, I know better than anyone else that you do not need support to break up with a guy." She sighs and pulls her keys from the ignition.

I slide out of the passenger's seat and gently click the door closed.

This time I might.

Beth slams her door.

"Hey, shhh," I whisper, my arms flailing around like I'm trying to catch the noise and hide it or something.

Last night, around this same time, after my shift at The Black Alcove, the bar I work at, I came here to surprise my boyfriend Jace—and, you guessed it, I caught him with another girl … naked. He doesn't know that I saw. His roommate, on the other hand, who owns the house and who happens to be Tyler Maron—my ex-best friend and the man who holds fifty percent of the blame on why my life turned out the way it did—caught me running to my car. I made him promise not to tell Jace. Which was easy, considering he's always trying to "repair our friendship," as he calls it.

Ugh.

Okay, tonight is not about me and Tyler. It's about Jace and what he deserves.

Revenge is way better than confronting him. Plus, when I think of it as revenge, I feel like it knocks my crazy factor down a notch. Which, technically, I don't think I'm crazy. I just prefer to show my emotions differently than others do.

"I'm just not sure how he's going to react," I say, and it's the honest truth. Most girls would go batshit insane on the other woman. Not me. In my mind, Jace is at fault here. He is the one in the relationship, and he is the one who should have said no.

I crouch down, pretending to rub my legs warm to be sure he doesn't see me and also so Beth doesn't catch on right away what I'm really up to. "Please come with me?"

"Fine," Beth groans. "But this better go fast, because Maverick is at home waiting for me."

Of course she brings up her fiancé. Every one of my

friends in Wind Valley has settled down but me. It's like a constant reminder of where my life should be right now. The worst part: in two minutes, I'm about to backtrack. Maturity isn't my strength these days. Well, not when it comes to making a decision for my own life, anyway.

Jace's lifted black and chrome truck is parked right out front, one tire propped up on the curb like your regular jack-ass. We have to walk past it to get to the front door.

This is it, Abby. Don't back out now.

"So, what are you … oh my god, what are you doing? Is that a knife? That thing is …" Beth stops mid-sentence when I jam a hunting knife into the back tire of Jace's truck.

"Ahh! Holy crap!" I scream whisper. I grab my right wrist as pain shoots toward my elbow and glare at Beth as the knife rattles off the sidewalk. Beth's bent over laughing.

"Did you plan for it to go *into* the tire?"

"Yes." I try not to laugh. "Now be quiet or they are going to hear you." I sneak a glance at the front window. No movement and the lights are still on. This is good.

I grab the knife and begin round two.

"Abby, stop, you can't be serious. You could get in trouble for this; *we* could get in trouble for this." She's got her hands on her hips now, acting like a total buzzkill.

"I'm extremely serious." I hike up my leg and immediately feel the handle of the knife through the bottom of my flip-flop. The knife doesn't budge. Gripping the bed of the truck, I pull myself up until I'm standing on his tire. Then, I repeatedly bounce on the knife—ignoring Beth, who is now tugging on the back of my shirt and yelling at me to get down —until I hear the smooth hiss of air leaking from the tire.

Success!

"Abby, get down. I hear someone."

My neck pops as I jerk it around at the familiar noise. Jace and Tyler are walking outside, talking loudly. Tyler's voice grows as if he were right next to me. I peek over the bed of the truck, and Tyler's eyes meet mine briefly. Then they do a double take.

"Man, let's wait another hour before we hit up the bar. It's early, no one goes this early."

"It's after ten, Tyler. How much longer do you want to wait?" Jace asks, continuing for his truck.

Shit!

I jump down and grab my knife, but as I pull back in what should be the segue into my quick getaway run—dramatic, smooth, commanding, just like in the movies—I'm jerked back.

Shit. Shit. Shit.

The knife is stuck.

"Abby, let's go!" Beth snaps at me. She's crouched behind the truck where they can't see her. "I cannot believe that I trusted that you were going to break up with him like a normal person. Let's go."

"I'm trying," I shush back, jerking again on the damn knife.

"Just leave it."

"It has my initials on it."

A gift from my mom for my eighteenth birthday. She knows me so well. *Not.*

"What the … seriously?" Beth moves around to the tire and pushes me out of the way. I duck when Jace's ball cap comes into view over the back of the truck. Then, Beth and I yank on the knife together.

Nothing happens.

"Let me drive!" Tyler shouts.

"Dude, what the fuck is your deal? It's my truck. I'll drive."

"But I'm thinking of getting one just like it, and I need to test drive something." Tyler's response is quick.

"Dude, whatever," Jace replies as I see the keys flying through the air, right before Tyler comes into view.

"What the fuck are you doing, Abby?" he says through the side of his lips. I barely see his mouth move.

"Trying to leave. What does it look like?" I whisper frantically.

"Whoops!" Tyler drops the keys. He kneels in front of the tire and jerks the knife out in one swift move.

Damn.

His white T-shirt hugs his bicep, and, oh boy, he looks good tonight. I mean, he's always had the whole Liam Hemsworth thing going on, but tonight he looks even hotter than a movie star. His hair is the perfect dirty blonde and his eyes are brightest green I've ever seen. Don't even get me started on his smile. Shoot, any girl would agree to whatever he wanted just to see it one more time. I would know. I've been that girl.

Tyler gives the knife to me and mouths "run." We don't hesitate in the slightest.

I tuck the knife into my back pocket as I duck to run. The tire is successfully slashed, and I'm not leaving any evidence of my crime at the scene.

Hunching behind her car, Beth shoots daggers from her

eyes as she stares at me. The look is so intense, I need something else to focus on.

Yes, this crack on the sidewalk is a nice distraction.

"I can't believe you," she seethes.

"It's fine. No one saw us but Tyler," I say just as Jace begins shouting a string of curses.

Jackass.

"I should have known you were going to do something crazy tonight. You made breaking up sound so simple," Beth adds.

I shrug and then we both hunker down tighter when the lights of Tyler's truck flash our way. I crawl around the front of the car and watch them turn the corner.

Then, I start to laugh.

Beth is still glaring at me. Only now she's standing with her hands on her hips and looking at me like my mom would when I'd come home past curfew, before she decided she didn't want anything to do with me.

The whole picture makes me laugh even harder. Slowly, Beth's lips begin to tug into a smile.

"You are out of control," she says and unlocks her car.

"There is nothing wrong with that," I tell her.

With the click of my seat belt, she pulls onto the road. "Back to the BA?" she asks.

I nod.

"Oh man," she says, releasing a long breath. "I forgot how quickly hanging out with you could go from a zero to a ten in less than five seconds."

"I like to keep it interesting."

"Yeah, but …"

"But what?" I ask.

"Doesn't it feel a bit … high school-ish?"

"No, he cheated on me. I think it's justified."

"Well, maybe if you dated someone who was not a jackass and who cared less about the fingerprints on his truck and more about say, opening a door for you, you would see it differently."

"Eh, I don't know."

"Come on, Abby. You'd rather keep doing this than have a real relationship? Settle down? Fall in love?"

It's not as easy as she makes it sound. She knows my life. I'm not exactly the type that screams "settle down with me and take me home to your mom." Shit, once I confess about my mom to the guy I'm dating, he usually disappears within a week.

"I'm not trying to be mean. I'm just saying, a situation like the one we just created makes me even more thankful that I have Maverick," she says.

I roll my eyes.

"You were so much cooler before you met him." I nudge her arm.

"Yeah, but I wouldn't trade anything for what I have now," she says.

"What, a fiancé?"

"Yes, but also good friends, a job I actually want to be at, and a life filled with happiness and love."

I nod slowly. "Are you the new spokesman for the Hallmark Channel?" I ask.

Beth shakes her head. "God, I have no idea how you do it."

"Do what?"

"Stay the same old Abby I've known since we graduated

high school. I mean, you've yet to date a guy who actually cares about you," she says just as her cell phone rings. She presses a button on the steering wheel and Maverick's voice fills the car.

I'm not the same old Abby.

I've changed.

Haven't I?

I cross my arms and stare out the window as we near the BA.

If I'm not at home, I'm at the BA. You'd think that since I work there, I'd never want to hang out there. You'd also think that, given my reputation, I wouldn't want to socialize with the people who spend their time there. I've hurt more than one of them and, yet, they still keep me around, which is just crazy because I've never …

Oh my god.

I glance over to Beth, who's still chatting away as she takes the last turn onto the bar's street.

I've never done anything except let them down. Whether it was my choices or actions, I haven't been a good friend. Or person in general, it seems.

Maybe Beth is right.

I'm the same old Abby.

My cell lights up with an incoming text. Tyler. I flip it over just as Beth says goodbye to Maverick.

"Do you think it's too late?" I ask her.

"For what?"

"To change."

She must gather that I'm referring to my life and not something lame like our clothes, because she doesn't answer right away.

She pulls into a parking space and turns off her car. "It's never too late," she says.

She shoots me wink before she gets out. I follow, but I don't think I'll go inside. My mind is racing from our short conversation.

I'll always wonder if, on that day, I'd found the strength to say no, to reject the boy I fell in love with at thirteen and who used to be my best friend, how different my life would be right now.

Maybe I'd still have all my girlfriends, and everyone who used to invite me to parties or movies wouldn't think of me as trouble. Maybe I'd have had a roommate those first couple years out of school rather than still living with my mom and maybe I wouldn't have … it doesn't matter. What's done is done, but what I do know is this: I need to make some changes.

Tyler

You only get one real best friend in life, and once you find them, you should do whatever you can to keep them.

Damn.

I wish someone had told me this right out of high school instead of letting me figure it out on my own.

The cell phone vibration in my pocket wakes me up enough to pay a bit more attention to the real estate meeting I'm in this morning. I'd like to blame my lack of energy today on staying out too late with Jace, since he's moving back to California today, but that's not it. I was thinking about Abby.

She was my best friend. Then I messed up. *We* messed up.

Every now and then, Abby and I can be civil, but

somehow it ends with us in an argument. We then don't speak for a while, I try to make it better, Abby has her quick, snappy responses, and eventually we start talking again … and start the process all over.

She has no idea how much I'd kill to regain the type of friendship we had growing up. She's the only person I trusted, and as crazy as it sounds, she still is.

I sit up straighter in my chair and glance around the room as I pretend to be taking notes. For the last three years, I've sold more homes than anyone sitting at this table. That includes Rob, and he's been here for almost a decade.

"Let's move on to our next topic," Marshall Jinks, my boss, says and flops open a giant, red, three-ring binder in front of him as he sits at the head of the rectangle table.

I'm glad they're changing the subject since I have no idea what the last one was. I really hope it wasn't anything that pertained directly to me.

"The office in Colorado."

Yes.

He's been talking about this location for months. He hasn't come right out and said it, but I'm pretty sure he's going to pick someone from this office to lead the new one.

It's a challenge I'm ready to accept. I've earned it. Each house I sell, I'm selling a family a fresh start. It's my turn, and moving to Colorado, or anywhere, and managing my own team is how that's going to happen. It's all part of my plan. Being my own boss and being in control is at the top of the list.

He's got my undivided attention. "As most of you know, I'd like to train the new agents in this office and move them to Colorado once the building is complete at the end of the summer. With only a few months till that deadline, it's time I share my plans with everyone."

Say you want someone from this office.

"I would like to promote one of my agents here to lead the Colorado office."

Yes! Fuck. Yes. If there weren't a group of people sitting near me, I'd definitely being doing a victory dance right now, but I'll have to settle for a clap with the rest of the group for now.

"Choosing this candidate isn't going to be an easy choice. There are many of you here who qualify for this position and who I would be honored to call my partner."

I survey the fifteen of us around the table. Who else could he be considering? I mean, Macy, maybe. She sold one only less house than me last year. Carl could be picked; he's really good at bringing clients in to the company, and Sandy—well, Sandy is the boss's sister-in-law.

"I'm not going to do a competition or something crazy to pick this person. Just continue working hard and remember that I notice all your hard work."

That's it?

"Now, next up," he says, and I lean back, the creak of my chair in unison with everyone else who clearly feels the way I do.

That's seriously all he's going to say about the promotion?

"We have a full schedule for company events over the next six weeks. As you all know, we market ourselves on our community involvement. I don't want the idea of a possible promotion to detour us from this."

How could it? Everyone could handle the company events

in their sleep. Park picnics, fancy dinners out, a work banquet. It's not like the company gets too crazy.

"This year, things are going to be a bit different." Again, Mr. Jinks has my full attention. "Along with a few of the same good ole times, we'll be hosting a fundraiser and going on a weekend getaway to a cabin near the Colorado office. A lot of that market is about the great outdoor living that the state has to offer, so I want to make sure everyone is fully prepared. I also want to introduce ourselves to the surrounding community in that region."

"You're bringing all of us?" Macy asks, her eyes roaming the room.

"Yes," he answers. "You're all my top agents, and it's time you are rewarded for it."

"That's … wow … this is a great idea. Genius," Carl says, and I want to roll my eyes. He's always kissing the boss's ass. Don't get me wrong—we all do it from time to time, but he's the worst.

To be honest, I'm the youngest of the bunch at twenty-five, and not to be stereotypical, but you'd think I'd be the one saying or doing cheesy shit to get the boss's attention. Lucky for me, I keep my age in mind and speak only after I've fully thought out what to say.

"Thank you, Carl." Mr. Jinks smiles proudly. "I really want us to stand out against the other agencies in town. If anyone has ideas, I'm open to them all."

"We could give something away," Macy says. "People are always drawn to free stuff."

"It could be something like a free shampoo cleaning with every purchase," Sandy chimes in.

Yeah, because every person would rather buy a brand-new

house than to just spend sixty bucks and hire someone to clean the carpets they already own.

"That's brilliant," Carl adds.

I hold up my pen as if I'm raising my hand. I hate to interrupt their *brilliant* idea.

"Tyler, do you have something to add?" Mr. Jinks asks.

"Not really," I say, and Macy glares at me. "I was actually thinking we could do something more personal for our clients."

I say the words carefully when what I really want to say is "something that doesn't bribe people to come to us."

"Go on."

"Everyone in Wind Valley knows we can sell them a house …"

"Obviously." Carl snickers and shakes his head. "Tell us something we don't know, Maron."

I side-eye Carl but don't reply. "What we should be doing is selling them a home. A life. A new beginning. Showing them that this house, a new house, is the start to family memories and years of happiness."

Carl, Macy, and Sandy stare at me. Sandy sits up straight in her chair and taps her pen on the table.

"I actually think his idea would be a better approach," she says.

"Yeah, but how do we do that?" Carl asks.

"Easy," Mr. Jinks cuts in, and all eyes are on him. "I want all the events this year to be family-oriented. Bring your wives, husbands, girlfriends, boyfriends, kids, brothers, whoever. Every event will be about family. I love it."

He begins to gather his notebook, cellphone, and snaps his pen into his front shirt pocket. "You've got quite the view on this market, Tyler. Don't let go of it," he says right before he walks out of the room.

All eyes turn to me briefly before most everyone takes their belongings and return to their offices. Carl stays behind to walk out with me.

"You are the last person I'd have expected to take the family route on this, Tyler," he says, lingering in the doorway and causing me to stop.

"Why is that?" I ask.

"Isn't it obvious?" His brows dip. Guess it's clear that it's not. "You're the only single guy at the firm, Tyler."

He smirks and, with an arrogant laugh, leaves me standing in the hall outside the conference room.

Did I just set myself up?

As I pass cubicle after cubicle down the hall to my office, I notice one thing: every person has pictures of their families on their desks.

I don't even own a dog. Shit.

If Mr. Jinks wants family and I don't have anyone other than my parents, well, maybe I need to change that. Maybe I need to get me a temporary something to get me through these events.

I take a seat behind my desk. Today's schedule is booked full. My performance will overlook my lack of family. I don't need to go getting crazy with a fake girlfriend.

"Tyler." Mr. Jinks pops into my office.

"Yes, sir?"

"I'm looking forward to meeting your other half." He grins. "I assume that's what sparked your sudden interest in family values."

So, as of this moment, I'm in a relationship.

"Yes, sure, she'll be thrilled to hear the news as well," I say.

Mr. Jinks slaps the doorframe and leaves.

Good.

My day just got even busier. I have houses to sell and a girlfriend to find.

CHAPTER TWO

Abby

My black, round, bar tray slides onto the counter as I wait for my newest table's drink order. Resting my hip against the bar top, I can't help but allow my gaze to linger to the far-right corner near the entrance. It's *their* table. It's where they always gather together when they come in to eat. The bar's floor-to-ceiling windows behind it reveal a bright view of downtown Wind Valley. The corner space is set up perfectly to combine two or three tables, which they almost always have to do. It's close to the jukebox and on a platform that provides the best view of the stage. It's the best table in the entire bar, and I've yet to be invited to sit with them. I only serve them while they are here. Which, given our history, makes sense.

I like to think that if Tyler and I hadn't drunk too much that night, I'd be a regular at that table with them. That I'd have years of memories instead of regrets. That I'd have all my girlfriends instead of only Beth. I love the girl, but the pressure as my only friend has to be high.

Luke, the BA's head bartender, places two drinks on my tray without a word. The lunch rush is starting to pick up, so there isn't much time for chitchat unless we want to fall behind. I mean, we don't exactly do a whole bunch of talking when it's slow, but we do work together, so Luke tolerates me.

Tray in hand, I head back to work, weaving through tables and customers.

I'm lucky. I know I shouldn't complain about my situation. I made the messy life I have, and now I have to either maintain the mess or clean it up.

I want to clean it up. I just don't see how it's possible. The damage I've caused the people closest to me … well, it's the exact reason they've never invited me to sit with them. Almost having a drunken threesome with Tyler while he was still dating Kelsey was just the start. I'd probably have gone through with it too, but he was out of condoms, and I'd reached my quota of bad choices for the night by just being there and walking around in my bra and panties.

Being drunk around the guy you've wanted to be with since you were a teenager was not good. I was selfish. He was more selfish. We both lost a lot that day.

"Is there anything else I can get you guys right now?" I ask, placing the vodka soda and rum and Coke in front of my two-top. The older, white-bearded, bald-headed man sips his auburn drink and his shoulders drop as he swallows.

"Nope, this is wonderful. Thank you, beautiful."

I nod, flashing my "I need a bigger tip" smile and head to the next table.

I live such an exciting life here in Wind Valley, and it's not going to get any better if all I do is dwell on my past. Which I do every day when I'm at work, watching those who used to be my best friends laugh and move on with their lives without me, and every night when I go home alone.

Again, it's all my fault. I was weak and thought it was a sure way to get him to finally fall for me.

I was wrong.

"Don't set your monkey on the floor." Kelsey's cheerful voice captures my attention as she steps inside the BA, picking up a stuffed animal next to her feet. Her light brown hair is braided to the middle of her back as she ushers her small kids, a boy and a girl, inside and to—you guessed it—the table.

I wave. "Hey, Kelsey."

"Hey, Abby," she says and points to the table where her husband, Ethan, is waiting. He's part owner of the bar. Both kids run to their father, and Ethan makes a growling noise combined with a few funny faces as their kids squeal into his arms with laughter.

"Is Sara here?" Kelsey asks.

"Not yet," I say, and she nods. Then she joins her family, kissing her husband in greeting.

Not to say that what I did was right in any way, but if it weren't for me, she and Ethan wouldn't be together.

"Hey, Abs," another voice calls out behind me. I don't even have to turn around to know who it is. That, and the fact he's the only person to ever use that ridiculous nickname, sends me in the other direction.

"Abby, stop, really?"

I keep walking.

"Abby."

I pass behind the storage room door that reads "employees only," needing a moment to adjust my emotions to the fact that he's here.

Except he doesn't give me that.

Tyler barges right through the door behind me.

"This is an employees only area, Tyler. I'd imagine with your whole fancy business degree you can not only read but process what those words actually mean."

"Oh, so you didn't lose your voice?"

"Oh, so you still don't know how to listen."

"We need to talk."

Nope.

His eyes narrow and his hands push back the sides of his suit so he can rest them on his hips as though he just read my mind.

"We really don't," I tell him and move to step around him. He sidesteps into my way.

"I don't have time for this, Abby. I'm on lunch and I need to get back to the office."

"Well, this is a wasted lunch hour."

"Are you ever going to just have a normal conversation with me?" he asks.

I shrug. "Probably not."

"Fine. I'll make this quick. Don't go slashing any more tires, and I need a favor."

I twist with a hand propped on my hip. "A favor? I'm standing here telling you to go away and you need a favor. Do you hear how messed up this sounds?"

"Yeah, but I don't care. You're the only person I trust."

You're the only person I trust.

I've heard that before. Right before I lost everyone closest to me.

I wait for him to go on, but before he can, his cell phone rings.

"Shit, I need to take this," he says. "Tyler Maron," he answers, then pulls the phone away to whisper to me, "Come by my place tonight when you're off, okay?"

I roll my eyes and shake my head. "I'm not into those types of favors, Tyler, and you should be very aware of who your roommate is and that I don't care to be anywhere in that area."

"Funny. You know Jace moved today."

"Ha, right," I say.

His glare softens.

He's serious.

Wow.

Jace is an even bigger jackass then I thought.

"I'm sorry, Abby. Please come by later," he says to me before he exits. When I step back into the bar, he's nowhere to be seen.

With a death grip on my purse strap and my focus on my steps —I do this anytime I come home—I head up the sidewalk to my apartment building. Although it might only be six o'clock now, the routine is no different. When I reach the main doors, I pause, take a breath, and then turn the knob as slowly as I can. If it makes even the slightest noise, my neighbor and landlord, Troy, will appear from his apartment on the ground floor, and that's the last thing I want.

After the slowest door opening and closing in history, I let go of the handle and turn for the stairs. Now, it's time to master the no-squeak steps. First step is good. Second step is even better. Third step would have been wonderful too if the girl who lives across from Troy hadn't just barged through the door. It slams behind her, and just as Troy opens his door, I dart up the steps.

"Abby!" he shouts, and I pause.

Damn it. So close.

"Your rent is late, again," he says, and I swear the scowl he gives me is so intense it's going to leave a mark between his eyes. His sweats, which look like they double as a napkin, hang loose under his naked beer belly. The one he's scratching as his dilated brown eyes watch me.

Rent is one of two reasons I wanted to avoid having to talk to him.

"I know, I …"

The girl who lives below me—whose name I've never cared to ask—opens her door and closes it as if she didn't see me or Troy.

"I've told you time and time again, pay your rent on time or we'll have to work out some other kind of deal." His eyes steadily roam my body, the way they always do when he makes this comment—which is every month for the last three months. Rent has been harder and harder to come by. I work almost every night, but someone else needs my money more than I do. I just need a few more months, that's it. Then everything will be okay.

"I'll get it for you," I say and turn for my door.

"You have twenty-four hours to give me this month's and next month's rent or you're out. Unless …"

The cheeseburger I ate for lunch spins in my stomach.

Without looking at my landlord, I nod.

"I'll get you your money," I tell him, but instead of going home to forget this encounter ever happened, I descend back down the steps.

Tyler said he needed a favor … well, so do I.

CHAPTER THREE

Tyler

"The backyard is perfect for birthday parties, swing sets, trampolines, you name it. Your kids will love it, and it's big enough for a putting green along the west fence, too," I say, flashing my best smile at the couple in front of me. Selling the first house after Mr. Jinks announced the promotion would be gold, and I'm just the man to get the job done.

The pale and brunette woman smooths a hand over her growing belly and grins up at her husband, who stands a good three feet over her.

He nods and kisses her forehead.

Her smile is beaming when she turns to me and says, "We'd like to put in an offer."

"That's wonderful." I give them the quick spiel of what happens next.

My leg tingles as I feel my phone buzz in my pocket; the temptation to turn away from potential new buyers to check it is strong. What if Abby is calling now instead of coming over later? I need a date for these functions, and I really don't see any other woman in this town who wouldn't think it's more than it is.

"Thank you," I tell the couple once more as they head for the door. "I look forward to speaking with you soon."

The woman smiles as she looks around the entryway once more. Then, they're gone, and I yank my phone out as if it will explode if I don't answer in the next five seconds.

I sigh and roll my eyes. Six new text messages—really, Carl?

Carl likes to text. Which is normally fine, but not Carl's style of texting.

Carl: Did they put in an offer?

Carl: I've got someone who wants to see the house.

Carl: Are you even working?

Carl: Tyler. This couple is waiting.

Carl: I just heard you have a girlfriend … is that true?

Carl: I'll squash the rumors now, just say the word.

Of course, he'd be willing to *squash* the rumors. He's willing to do anything that makes him look like the winner.

I send him a quick text—*yes, an offer was made*—and then shove my phone back in my pocket. I pack up the pamphlets I made for the house and lock up on my way out before I head back to the office.

I'll get this offer submitted and then work on what I'm

going to say to Abby. For some reason, just straight-out asking if she'll be my fake girlfriend sounds crass and insulting. Or at least, asking it from Abby would be. We've never had a relationship beyond strictly friends.

There was this one time, when I cheated on my then-girlfriend Kelsey. I'd only done it that once, which doesn't justify it, but that day, Abby and I almost took our friendship too far. That whole day was messed up. I'd been drinking when Abby came over to hang out. My neighbor, Jennifer, had dropped by to share the weed she'd just bought and after about an hour, the opportunity for a threesome came up and … I was an idiot.

Have to learn somehow, right?

I pull around the corner to the firm and park my truck in a spot up front.

Carl and Macy are huddled near the elevators when I walk in.

"Tyler, perfect, you're here," Carl calls out, leading Macy to face me. "I was just telling them about your mystery girlfriend." His grin stretches wide. "Tell us about her."

"Yeah, I never knew you were seeing someone," Macy says, crossing her arms and smirking at me. "Do spill."

These two are the number one reason why my working at the Colorado office would be so much better than being here.

"I like to keep my personal and professional life as separate as I can," I tell them and then point to the elevator doors. "Excuse me."

"But you've never once mentioned her," Carl starts. "I mean, this morning you didn't even correct me when I said you were single."

The doors open and I step inside, hitting both the third floor button and the one to close the doors quickly.

"It's not necessary for you to know the correct details of my life, Carl. Now, if you'll both excuse me, I have some work to finish up for the day." I barely get the words out before the doors close and I'm safe from the high school kids I apparently work with.

"My husband can't wait to come," I hear another coworker say to Mr. Jinks as I reach my floor. "He's really looking forward to meeting everyone."

"That's wonderful, Annie. The Mrs. was also thrilled to hear the new plans."

Shit.

What in the hell did I create with this stupid idea? How are people really this excited to bring their family to work events?

"Tyler, just the man I wanted to see. Did you get an offer on the Wolcott house?" Mr. Jinks asks when he spots me.

"I did," I say and sport a smile. This will make the third house I've sold this week if the offer is accepted.

"Splendid. This day is just getting better and better. The event schedule should be in your inbox. We'll talk soon," he says, nodding his departure.

"How happy are you to bring your other half to these events?" Annie asks me.

"Super excited," I tell her and try to give her my best enthusiastic smile.

"Me too. I finally get to show off my new husband. I can't wait," she says, her focus now on her left hand as she heads down the hall.

Is that why everyone is excited? To show off their families? Shit … is family going to be a competition too?

Does just having a girlfriend sound too … childish?

Damn it. I screwed myself so bad on this one.

Okay, so maybe Abby needs to be more than just a girl on my arm. She needs to have a real fake place in my life. One that means I'm serious. That I'm a family guy.

Engaged screams family guy, right?

Shit. What am I even thinking? I need to talk to Abby first before I start making up any more about this relationship I don't actually have.

What if she doesn't want to go along with it? What if I can't find anyone to play this part?

I shake the thought and turn on my computer. A few clicks later and I've placed the offer and pending review. Next, I open my email and pull up the event schedule Mr. Jinks mentioned.

There are six main events, with a few quick employees-only meetings in between. First up, our annual picnic in the downtown square. It's not just our firm that attends—most local businesses do too. It's a great way to network without actually talking business. Second up is a dinner at Mr. Jinks's property at the base of the mountain. Third is the Colorado resort over the July Fourth weekend. After that, a meet-the-new-staff brunch at the firm's address, the education fundraiser, and lastly, the end-of-summer barbeque bash. In parentheses after barbeque, it reads: Colorado leader announced after dessert.

Six events. This should be easy. I shut down my computer and stuff my laptop in my bag before I head out the door to my truck.

If everything goes as planned tonight, I'll have a little less stress, a new fiancée, and a career that's right on track.

I need Abby to say yes so badly, I'll do whatever it takes until she agrees.

Tyler and Abby Maron … it has a nice ring to it.

It's a little scary how desperate I am to receive this promotion, but the best things should scare you, right?

CHAPTER FOUR

Abby

I love the smell of rain. Or in this case, soon to be rain. Something about it feels … clean. Like, it doesn't matter what kind of day it's been, the rain will wash it all away and the day can start over. Cool, calm, and refreshed. *New.*

Much like I'm hoping my life will be, as soon as Tyler shows up.

How long does one have to sit on cold cement before they lose all feeling in their rear end? I'm about to find out.

At the same time, sitting outside on the front steps in the wind—although my hair is likely creating as many knots as it possibly can—is way better than going home to wait for Tyler to get off work.

The taste in my mouth goes sour just thinking about being at my apartment.

I wish I could say I know how I get myself into these situations, but that's a lie. I wanted a cheap apartment and, boy, did I find one.

A kid rides his bike in front of me as his father, I assume, jogs next to him. Sometimes I think my life would be different if my dad had stuck around. Maybe I wouldn't be sitting here right now, desperate to help Tyler with whatever favor he needs. Maybe I'd know the right way to act around guys. Maybe my lack of a father figure is why I've haven't dated anyone longer than six months.

That last theory sounds so textbook. I know the real reason not a single relationship has ever worked out. Tyler. He's the reason. It gets easier the less we are around each other—heck, just being here right now creates hundreds of memories and emotions that flood back.

It also makes me recognize I haven't changed as much as I thought I had.

Come on, Abby, you not a teenager anymore. You need to get over Tyler.

Perhaps part of the new me can be someone who isn't still pining over her childhood crush. I mean, why not? I should start a list of things to change. First can be Tyler. It makes sense. If I learn how to stop thinking of him as more than a friend, it should be easier to be kind to him and actually be his friend.

And friends help each other out when they need it. Hence, whatever Tyler needs me here for today.

I really hope this favor is along the lines of something lame like "hey, water my plants for a week while I'm gone." Then again, I need it to be a bigger favor than that to negotiate what I need. Or maybe not. He says I owe him, but really, I think he owes me for life. He's the reason I lost all of my girl-friends. Of course, I never denied the story that we'd slept together, he'd fed Kelsey even though it wasn't true. It was a shitty choice to get myself in that position, but sex and no sex are totally different outcomes.

Huh. Maybe new me should stop holding this grudge against him. After all, it was my choice to just go with it.

Then again, he was a shitty friend to ask it of me in the first place.

Damn. New me is going to be hard to get along with.

"Holy shit, am I glad to see you," Tyler says and grabs my hand to help me up. "Let's get inside."

The musk scent he wears surrounds me. I try not to look obvious as I take a breath. God, the white shirt he's unbuttoned at the collar, his tie hanging loose, is a sinful look on him. I can't even think about the way his gray slacks look over his butt. Junior high and high school Tyler was hot, but grown-up Tyler is bad for my health.

Damn it, Abby.

With another deep breath, I pull myself together and, just for safe measure, I say, "I'll start by saying I'm swearing off men, so if your favor has anything do with—"

"It doesn't." He shakes his head. "You seriously think that's what I want from you?"

My cheeks warm as I look past him. I mean, why not? But also ... thank you.

"Then, what do you need?"

"Let's go inside first," he says, brushing off my question. He holds up a plastic grocery bag when I don't answer.

"What's that?"

"Back up," he says with a sly grin.

I reach for the bag, but he jerks it back. "Nope, not till you come inside so we can talk."

"Tyler ..."

"Fine. I guess I'll just have to eat all these macaroons by myself."

Damn it. My favorite type of cookie.

"Ugh," I groan, letting my chin drop as I head for his door.

"Good. I'm hungry, and I want to say this in the correct way so that you say yes." His voice shakes a little.

"Well, that sounds reassuring," I grumble and pull up a seat at his kitchen island. Tyler's house has always been one I admired. It's three bedrooms and all one floor, which I think is genius. It's newly remodeled, and even though I enjoy every room, the kitchen is my favorite. I think it's the slate counter-tops and pale blue memory foam stools that hooked me.

"Trust me, it isn't as bad as you think," he says.

I let his words sink in. My mother told me that exact thing, the time she brought home another random guy and he didn't want me there. In my own apartment. My mother wanted whatever he had to offer more than she wanted me, and I had nowhere to go. I'll never forget running into Kelsey's brother, Conner, and feeding him some story about being dumped and needing a place to crash. I mean, come on, who wants to tell people her mother is a slut who kicked her daughter out, so she could get laid?

"Sure," I say and fumble through my purse for some hand lotion. Any distraction from that memory, no matter how little, will help. Especially when I think back to how I acted once I was in Logan and Conner's apartment. I walked around in my underwear, for crying out loud. In front of people who were just trying to help me, and all I did was make things worse.

But whatever.

I'm changing.

I can do this.

"Everything okay?" Tyler asks, setting a box of spaghetti noodles on the counter and looking me in the eyes.

"Yep," I say, fighting the tears.

My mother hasn't been the best mom—she's put me in some bad situations—but she's the only family I have. Which is why I'm sitting in Tyler's apartment right now.

"Is this about Jace?" he asks, and I scoff.

"No."

"But he—"

"Jace and I were over way before he cheated on me and way before he clearly planned to move to another state without telling me."

I'm also pretty sure Jace telling me he loved me the night before he cheated was probably his last attempt to get me to sleep with him. It didn't work. Surprise. I don't actually sleep around, contrary to what others might believe.

Tyler nods slowly. "All right. Abby, you can talk to me, you know," he says with a weak smile. His eyes hold my gaze, and it's like he knows I'm keeping something from him. Which, if anyone is going to know I'm hiding something, it's Tyler. He knows what kind of mother I had. He just doesn't know what kind of mother she's turned into.

"I don't want to talk about it. I want food, yes, but first I want to know why I'm here," I change the subject.

"Can't we—?"

"Tyler, just tell me already."

"Fine." He sighs and reaches into the fridge for some hamburger. "I need you to play my girlfriend at a few work events," he says, and I laugh. I full-on, belly shake, laugh. I laugh so hard my eyes start to water.

Play fake girlfriend to the guy I used to imagine myself settling down with—talk about setting myself up for heartbreak. No thanks. God, I forgot how funny Tyler could be.

My smile fades when I see his head drop with a long sigh.

He's not joking.

"What? Are you crazy?" I ask.

I can see the desperation in his eyes.

"Dead serious. There is a promotion up for grabs. I'm gathering that my boss wants a family man, and of all the things I have, a significant other is the one thing I don't."

"Tyler, this is—"

"Insane, I know, but I want this promotion, Abby. You're the only woman I know who won't freak out and want it to become the real thing."

"Okay …"

What girl doesn't want the real thing?

"It's only for six weeks and six events, to be exact." He presses his hands together. "I really want this."

I sigh.

"Please, Abby," he whispers and covers my hand with his own. "Please."

The gesture is like someone squeezing a stress ball and the stress ball is my heart.

What happens if I say no? Will he ask someone else? I close my eyes and take a deep breath. I don't think I can handle seeing him with another woman right now. Every time he dates, I date, and I just don't think that's wise for someone who is turning over a new leaf right now. So …

"You're sure you want to lie to everyone you work with?"

I know firsthand how being a dishonest person can end. I'm not sure this is something he can handle.

"Positive."

"And you'll take care of any backlash if this goes south?"

"Yes, but there won't be."

I could give it a go. As long as I don't let myself overthink everything, I should be fine, right? After all, when I compare a fake romance to having to deal with my landlord again, is there really a reason I haven't said yes to Tyler yet?

Yeah, because you're changing, and playing fake girlfriend will not help.

But doing this favor for him earns a favor for me, and that would get me one step closer to the new Abby. So technically ...

"All I have to do is play your girlfriend?" I ask.

He breaks eye contact and his mouth scrunches up.

"Tyler ..."

"I need you to be my fiancée," he says

My jaw drops.

What the hell did I just walk into?

I press my palms into my eyes and take a deep breath.

New Abby, I sure as hell hope you've got your shit together.

Tyler

I'd expected as much of a reaction. I just didn't plan for how I would respond to her evident shock.

"I don't know about this," she says and hops off her stool. With her hand covering her forehead, she paces between my kitchen and living room.

"I know, but I need them to see that I'm serious," I tell her.

"Uh, yeah, seriously lying."

"They don't need to know that."

"This is just too crazy. Even for me," she says.

"I'll do anything you want," I say when she turns for the door.

"Anything?" She pauses a few steps from the kitchen table.

"Yes, anything."

"Fine, I'll do it on one condition."

"Name it and it's yours."

"Your vacant rental, on Washington Road, is mine for the next six months, rent free."

"That's pretty specific." I laugh. "I have a feeling you had this planned. Plus, six weeks versus six months is …"

Her left brow peaks.

"Why rent free? What's the rent got to do with it?" I ask.

"Do you want me to play your fiancée or not?"

This is a property I own, and I won't need to seek approval from the firm, so I nod.

"It's yours," I say and keep my gaze on hers. What doesn't she want me to know?

"Great!" Her smile grows wider than I've ever seen, and she returns to her spot at the island. "Now, are you going to finish cooking? I'm starving."

I can't help but laugh as I, too, return to the kitchen. Abby shrugs off her jacket and when she does so, the sleeve on her shirt slips off her skin, revealing a crazy boney shoulder. I pause and stare because I've never seen a collarbone stick out that far on anyone I know.

She moves to hang her coat on the coat rack near the door, and I don't miss the way her shorts hang loosely off her hips. Have I been so focused on myself and my career that I missed whatever is going on in Abby's life right now?

I mean, the answer is obviously yes, but how can I get her to tell me about it?

"Why are you staring at me?" she asks, pausing in the living room.

I shake my head. "Sorry, I must have zoned out."

"Hey, if you decide to back out on the deal, I still get to keep that apartment, okay." It's not a question. "In fact, let's just shake on it now so I know you won't screw me over."

Screw her over? I would never do that.

I reach my hand out, and it doesn't get past me how her soft small hand fits in mine. We shake and then she smiles.

"Well, get on with the food."

"You bet," I say. I put the water on to boil and then find something for us, mainly her, to snack on while we wait.

She doesn't even question the fact that I just placed chips and salsa, an odd appetizer for spaghetti, in front of her. She just digs in, moaning with every bite. The sound both annoys me and turns me on.

"So what's the deal with this promotion? Why do you want it so bad?" she asks.

I shrug. "I just do."

"That's not a real answer."

"Well, I guess to start, I'd be my own boss," I tell her.

"Ah, say no more. It all makes sense now," she says with a small laugh.

"What does that mean?"

"It's just a typical Tyler move to make."

"Um …"

"You like to be in control. You like leading the situation. Or however you want to say it. If you make the rules, you know what to expect. You've never been the kind of person to enjoy spontaneity."

"Full-on lies. I just asked you to be my fake fiancée. That's at the top of the spontaneity list," I say.

"Yeah, it's the first time."

"And probably the last." She's right. I'm not a fan of the unexpected. I like knowing when and where and what is happening before it happens.

"Should we set some ground rules for this thing?" she asks between bites.

"Like what?" I ask.

"Tyler, I can't just show up and play fiancée out of nowhere. We need … rules or guidelines, if you'd rather use that word."

She's got a good point.

"Okay, what have you got in mind?" I ask.

"I don't know." She munches on a chip. "Do we always hold hands? Are we huggers? Do we say we don't like PDA and never touch in front of people? Do you want people to know I work in a bar or—?"

"I think I get where you're going with this now," I say. "I didn't think that far ahead. I figured I needed you to say yes first."

"True. So, you said it is only six events?" she asks.

I grab my cell and pull up the email. "Yes, all weekends," I say, and her face scrunches up. "What?"

"I need my weekends at the bar, Tyler. I make the most money on those nights."

"Yeah, but if you're not paying rent, you don't need …" My words trail off at the worried expression in her eyes. "I'll compensate the nights you miss."

She shakes her head. "I can't take your money, too, Tyler."

"Well, I really need you to do this for me, so you'll take whatever I want to give you."

She tugs on her bottom lip with her teeth for a moment then nods. I can't stop staring at her lips. Has she always been a lip biter?

"Tyler?"

"Yeah?"

"The water is boiling."

Shit. Pay attention to what you're doing, man.

"Okay, so guidelines." I try to redirect my mindset. I shouldn't be thinking about her lips.

"Okay, I think we should be hand-holders," she says.

I laugh.

"Hey, laugh all you want, but I think hand-holding means affection in a family-rated way, Tyler. We can't be all over each other, because that doesn't scream appropriate for picnics and barbeques. Hand-holding is sweet and gentle."

Another good point.

"Okay, we're hand-holders. Are we supposed to kiss?" I ask. *Seriously, Tyler. Stop with the lips already.*

"Hmm, we can be cheek-kissers."

"Cheek-kissers?" I ask.

"Yeah, whenever we greet each other or say good-bye, we kiss the other on the cheek. It's simple and, again, a family-friendly affection."

"Have you done this before?" I ask.

"Just watched a lot of movies." She laughs. "Although, I'll make some slight changes because almost all of them end with the couple falling in love, and we both know that isn't going to be the case here. Do you have paper, so we can write this down?"

That isn't the case here.

I know I said I wanted someone who wasn't going to grow attached, but damn, she was quick to rule me out.

I open my junk drawer and hand her a notepad and a pen.

"Do we have nicknames?" she asks as she scribbles down what we've already covered.

"You already have one. Abs. Do you think I need one, too?" I ask.

Abby sighs. "Tyler, I need real answers. You want this job. How do you want us to be represented as a couple?"

"I want us to be happy and fun and chill, and I want us to look like the best damn couple so that everyone envies us and sees the potential a team like the two of us can bring."

"So, you want us to look like we have a love that can't be broken. Got it." She again writes something down.

"What are you writing now?"

She shrugs. "I wrote 'Abby can't say cuss words.'" She laughs.

"You hardly ever cuss."

"That you know of. This is the longest conversation we've had without fighting in years, sooo ..."

She's right.

"Okay, so what's next?" I ask. Abby seems to be ready to jump into this position, and I couldn't be more thankful. Especially since right now, it feels like my best friend is back.

"We eat, and then I have a few things I need to take care

of, is what's next. Starting with moving out of my current apartment," she says, almost yanking the bowl of food in my hand away from me.

"I'll help," I say, and the noodles in her mouth almost fall back into the bowl as she shakes her head.

"That's okay. I can do it on my own. Thanks, though."

"I want to help. Who else are you going to ask?"

"It's really fine."

"Abby."

"Tyler."

She's the only person who can make me cave with just a look, so I nod. But I need to put my foot down.

"I'm helping, and I won't let you tell me no again."

"Tyler, I …"

I rest my hand on her leg. Our gazes fall to the touch. I've touched Abby before. Many times. However, this time it's different. This time I have the urge to run my hand up her legs and touch her in a way I never have.

She lets out a long breath and then crosses her legs, forcing my hand to fall from her body.

We eat in silence.

"I'll call you when I'm ready for your help, okay?" she says and heads for the door.

"Okay, I'll clear out the back seat of my truck so I'm ready."

"Okay" is all she says.

"Abby," I call out once more.

She spins, her brows rising as she waits for me to go on.

I glance to the cookies still in the bag hanging off a barstool, and her gaze follows my line of sight.

Snatching up the bag, she doesn't look back before she closes the door behind her.

We went from normal us to a better us to an awkward us all within an hour. I know she's hiding something. If she doesn't want to tell me right now, fine, but we're about to spend a lot of time together and, eventually, I will find out.

After all, from this moment on, she's my fiancée.

CHAPTER FIVE

Abby

My hands shake and my steps stumble as I make my way down the hall. Blue and white lockers and yellow benches line the walls. Some lockers are tall and skinny, some are wide and short, split with one over the other. I clutch the paper with my locker number and combination closer to my chest. Please let me get a tall and skinny one.

The halls are filled with parents and kids touring the school. Only one more week till I'm officially in junior high. I'm excited to get to leave home for most of the day but terrified I'll have to figure this all out on my own. Students around me are staring. I'm certain I'm the only one here without their parents.

I spot my locker and press my lips together to keep from frowning. It's a split locker, and it's on the bottom. I crouch down and try out my combo. It doesn't open. Six more attempts and watching two other kids cheer with their own accomplishments, I groan.

"Took me a few times, too."

The voice above me startles me, but then I look into a pair of bright green eyes, and any sadness I felt today has vanished. He grins at me, and I'm pretty sure I just fell in love at thirteen.

"I'm Tyler," he says, squats down to my height. He points to the combo in my hand with another grin that leaves me speechless. I hand him the paper.

"Okay, so to clear it, spin it a few times and then land on zero. Then, turn right to the first number, left for the second, and back to the right for the third without stopping." His finger presses the latch and my locker pops open. "If you let it stop, it'll lock back up and you'll have to keep starting over."

"Thanks," I say, finally finding my words. Or in this case, word.

"No problem. I'm in the locker above you, so I'll be around to help."

"Cool," I say. He just keeps smiling at me.

"What's your name?" he asks.

"Abby."

"Well, Abby," he begins and then twists around like he's looking for someone. "Let's check this place out before my parents come back. I don't want to be the kid who has his parents show him where everything is. Where are your parents?"

"I ditched them," I say without hesitation.

"Perfect," he says, grabbing my hand and slamming my locker shut as he pulls me down the hall.

He looks over his shoulder at me, and I can't stop smiling.

I shake the memory from my mind and pack the picture of

Tyler and me from seventh grade that sparked it in the first place. I doubt he knows I even have it.

I tape the box closed. The days where when no one knew anything about me were the best. Plus, Tyler … god, he was the best friend I've ever had.

"Knock, knock," Beth says as she steps inside my apartment. "You ready?"

"Yes." I push the box to the corner as I grab my purse. "You think this will be okay? I mean, I don't know if she even likes me."

"First of all, it's fine. Second of all, you and Skylar barely know each other. And third, you're a paying customer. She'll love you once she gets to know you."

"Even though she's friends with Kelsey?"

"Honestly, yes. Kelsey is so far past the whole thing with you and Tyler. For Christ's sake, she's freaking married and has children."

No matter how many times I'm reminded or how much time passes, I'll always feel like shit about that day. She was a good friend to me and I messed up.

"Yeah, okay." I wish I'd never have started this particular conversation.

I hop into Beth's car, and we make our way to the salon.

"I'm seriously stoked right now," she says, smiling at me.

"Why? Please don't be weird about it," I tell her.

"Um, because it's been years since you've been a brunette or had short hair."

The moment Tyler told me what he imagined our fake relationship would be like, I knew it was time to color and cut off my dead, bleached hair. Being blonde was fun, but it's time to look the part. Besides, it's just hair, and if I want to change it back, I can.

It's all part of the changes I'm making. I want to be happy, too, damn it. I just hadn't realized how badly I wanted it until Tyler was listing off the type of couple he wanted us to be. It's the exact love I can only dream of.

Beth pulls into the parking lot where Skylar works. Well, she actually owns the place. Skylar's family has money, but yet she chooses to work every single day. She and her fiancé, Luke from the BA, also own the best bookstore in town. To say those two are ambitious would be spot on. If I had a guy in my life, like a real one who wasn't shitty, I wonder what word people would use to describe us.

"What made you decide to change your hair anyway?" Beth asks. Her hair, which is the softest shade of red I've ever seen, is tied into a bun on her head instead of falling to the middle of her back like normal. She's got an appointment too, and we decided to do lunch and make a day of it.

"Umm." The deal Tyler and I have is going to make people go nuts. I'll be the first to admit this decision isn't among my best. And sharing it? Well, that doesn't exactly scream I'm trying to make a change.

I suck at this.

Plus, I don't want word getting around to take away any chance of promotion for Tyler. The desperation in his eyes was so familiar. That look made my toes curl, and I hated seeing it.

"It's just time to start working on me," I finally say.

She nods as I hold the door for her.

"Well, I can honestly say that if this is part of your 'is it too late to change?' comment in my car the other night, I am so freaking onboard, it's not even funny."

Although she said it's not funny, she still cracks a smile.

So do I.

Skylar welcomes us both, and her kindness instantly calms me. I take the seat in her chair and take a deep breath.

Abby James 2.0, here we go.

* * *

Turns out, moving an entire apartment by yourself is hard work. Like crazy hard. I'm not just saying that because I'm pinned between my mattress and the wall right now. The nightstand dropping on my pinkie toes was the first sign.

"Shit," I mumble to myself. If I had made an effort to get to know my neighbors, maybe I wouldn't have to do this alone. If I weren't a big ole scaredy-cat, I'd have called Tyler like I said I would. But I don't want to chance Tyler and Troy running into each other. I don't have to be a genius to know that wouldn't end well.

I push the cushion away from me and wiggle out from under it as my phone rings.

Tyler. Of course. It's been three days since I agreed to be his fiancée, and I've only seen him once to get the key to my new place.

"Hey, Tyler," I answer. "I'm just about to clock in at work. Can I call you later?"

"You're here?" he asks. "I just stopped in for lunch."

Shit.

"Oh, I'm—"

"Get that damn mattress off my staircase!" Troy's voice echoes off the silent stairwell, and I cringe.

"Abs," Tyler says slowly. "What are you *really* doing?"

"I'm …"

"Don't lie to me," he says before I get the chance.

"Fine. I'm moving my stuff to my new apartment," I say. "So I'll call you later."

I hang up before he can say anything else. Even if I had lied to him, we both know Tyler is going to show up here any moment. Which means I need to sweet-talk Troy into going back inside his apartment.

"Hey, Troy, sorry. I'll have this out of here in just a sec. Anything else you want me to do before I'm out?"

His head jerks back and his lips shake like he doesn't know what to say.

"Just hurry it up" is what he comes up with. His door closes, and I rest against the wall. That was easier than I thought.

Now, back to this damn mattress.

Finding my balance, I grip one side and pull it toward me as I step backward down the steps. Pushing it and watching it ride the stairs was my first options, but I can't afford to break anything. Step by step, I make progress.

See, I don't need anyone.

"Jesus," Tyler says, walking through the door. I hadn't expected him to show up so quickly; I miss a step. I let go of the mattress to catch my balance, but the queen-sized bed doesn't plan on stopping.

"Fuck!" he shouts, leaping in front of me to stop the mattress before it crushes me against the wall.

When everything stops and there is no noise, I smile at him.

"What the hell?" he asks me.

"I—" is all I get out before, surprise, Troy reappears from his apartment.

"I told you to cut the bullshit, girl," he says.

Tyler's neck pops when he turns to face my landlord. "Don't speak to her like that."

"Tyler, it's fine. Let's just move the bed."

"I'll speak to her however the fuck I want, kid. Maybe if she paid rent, I'd be nicer, but she hasn't for two months now."

Tyler's eyes meet mine, but I look away quickly.

"Yeah, that's what I thought," Troy goes on. "Now hurry your pretty little ass up."

"Dude, I told you not to speak to her like that." I tug on Tyler's arms to turn away his attention, but he doesn't even notice.

Troy scowls as he takes a step toward Tyler. "Who the hell do you think you are?"

"Her fiancé. So I'd really appreciate it if you'd treat her with respect."

"Her fiancé," Troy repeats and laughs in Tyler's face. "She didn't mention no fiancé when she in my bed the other night."

Tyler grunts. "Doubtful."

"She didn't."

"I meant doubtful that she was in your bed," he clarifies.

"You don't think I could get a fine piece of …?"

Troy doesn't get to finish the thought before Tyler's right fist connects with his face.

"What the hell!" Troy shouts, punches his door, and then lands a hit on Tyler. It wasn't as hard as Tyler's, but still, this escalated quickly.

"Whoa, whoa!" I shout and try to wiggle my way in to separate them while avoiding getting myself punched. If I don't stop this, there is good chance I won't be able to get the remainder of my stuff from upstairs, and the last thing I want is for the cops to show up. With my luck, Tyler's dad would be on patrol, and it's safe to say neither of us wants that.

But Troy and Tyler aren't budging.

"Tyler!" I shout.

He stumbles back and Troy catches his breath.

"I want you out of this building now!" he yells.

"Okay. Yes," I say. "I just have a few more things, ten minutes, tops."

"If I step out of my apartment one more time and find this piece of—" Troy keeps his gaze on Tyler, but I know he's talking to me.

I press my hand against Tyler's chest to stop him.

"I need my stuff," I growl.

"Five minutes," Troy says and slams his door.

"Let's get you out of here." Tyler takes the stairs two at a time.

I let out a breath.

I know I should be focused on getting my stuff, but Tyler just punched someone in the face for me. He stood up for me. The way friends do.

He looked damn good doing it, too.

I'll worry later about how I shouldn't be thinking about him that way anymore. Right now, I'm getting my best friend back.

. . .

Tyler

"Ouch. Shit, don't press so hard."

Abby sighs and lifts the ice pack off my eye. "I'm not pressing hard; you're just being a baby," she says. When she moves to put the ice back on my face, I wiggle out of her reach, sitting up on the couch.

"I'm not a baby. That guy just got in a lucky shot."

"A lucky shot, is that what you're calling it?"

"Yeah."

Another sigh, but this time a smile follows. "I can't believe you punched him in the face," she says.

"I can't believe you lived above a guy who clearly had no respect for you."

"I can't believe he hit you back."

I chuckle. "I can't believe that last part either or the fact that he left us alone while we finished moving your stuff."

"I think it helped that I only had the box spring and bed frame left." Abby slaps the Ziploc full of ice into my hand. "Keep this on your eye. It's still swelling."

I do as she says, trying my best not to wince at the cold bag.

"You know, the whole thing could have been avoided if you had just called me in the first place." I pin her with a "you know I'm right" look.

Abby groans. "I was doing just fine."

"That's not the point." I lean back into her couch. "I never thought you couldn't handle it. I just wanted to help."

Her tongue slips out to wet her lips as she tucks loose hair behind her ear.

Truth be told, when I stepped through that door and saw her, when I said *Jesus*, I wasn't referring to the mattress. For a split moment, the Abby I grew up with was standing right there in front of me, her blue eyes sparkling against her complexion, framed by her dark hair. She looked so ... her. It was also that moment I realized that talking hasn't been our strength, and I hardly know the woman she's become.

I clear my throat. "Why did you change your hair?"

Her hand immediately reaches to her short locks. "Oh, it was time for something new. Plus, I want to look the part for you and your chances for this promotion."

"You didn't have to change anything," I tell her. Shit. I hope I didn't give her that impression. She's perfect just the way she is.

"I did, and I need to change more than just my hair, but the rest will take time."

"Can I ask you something?" Hopefully, she doesn't say no and find an excuse to leave. Then again, we're sitting on her couch in her new apartment, so she wouldn't get very far.

"If it's about why I'm living here or why I was living there, no. Anything else, yes." She tilts her head just enough to look me in the eye.

I lower the ice pack.

"Why don't we hang out anymore?"

She grunts. "What do you call what we're doing now?"

"Abs," I say and scoot closer to her. "You know what I mean."

"I ..." she starts, crossing her arms and leaning back. "We grew apart. Simple as that."

"Yeah, but—"

"Tyler, why does it matter?" She moves to the kitchen

table and starts unloading the mail she stuffed into her purse before we left. "We're talking again now."

"Because it does." I move to stand next to her. I want her to look at me. I want her to see that I truly do care. "You were my best friend and somehow, one day, I saw you only when things went wrong."

"We got drunk and almost had sex, Tyler," she snaps. "Don't act like you don't know what changed us."

Shit. I walked right into that one.

I shift on my feet and then meet her gaze. "We've never talked about it … till this moment," I say.

"Yeah, well, I thought ignoring it would make up for my betrayal to Kelsey, but it didn't, so …"

I place my hand over hers as she leans on the table. I open my mouth to tell her how sorry I am, but then she looks down and I follow her stare. An envelope from DeerHorn Rehab Center.

My gaze darts to hers, but I can't gauge her expression because she already sliding the mail under her purse and moving away from me.

"I'm actually pretty tired. I think we should call it a night," she says.

"Abby …"

"Tyler, really, just let it go."

"I can't let it go," I snap, causing her to step back. "I'm sorry. I just, I want us to get back to that. I want my best friend back."

To this, she nods. "Friends, right. I do too, but these things don't happen overnight."

I nod, slowly. The exhaustion in her eyes is a sign not to pry more.

"Fine," I say, handing her back the ice pack. "I'll see you on Saturday for the annual picnic. Meet me by the west-side tables?"

"Okay."

I want to say more, and I have no idea where the strength to not do just that comes from. She might be my fake fiancée but she'll always be my best friend. Whatever she's hiding from me, I'm going to make her see that she can trust me again, and then I'm going to fix whatever is going wrong.

* * *

The ball bounces off the rim.

"That's the third time you've missed that shot," Logan says as he chases after the ball now rolling onto the indoor track that surrounds the gym's basketball court.

He passes the ball back to me, and I attempt the shot again.

Fuck.

"You want to tell me what's up?" he asks.

I shake my head. "If I knew, I'd fix it, and then you'd be losing instead of ahead by three shots."

He chuckles as my ringtone goes off from inside my bag. I jog to it and pull out my phone.

It's a number I don't recognize. More than likely a potential buyer. I should probably call them back, but I'm clearly not on my game right now.

"Expecting a call?" Logan asks.

"No, I just thought maybe it was Abby," I say and drop my cell back into the bag.

"Oh," he says. "Are you two on speaking terms again?"

I nod. "Yeah."

Growing up, there was a time you couldn't get me, Abs, Logan, Kelsey, Sara, and Beth to separate. We did everything together, and if anyone knows my relationship with Abby as well as I do, it's Logan.

"Is that a good idea?" he asks.

"Why wouldn't it be?"

"Um," he begins, the ball flying through the air as he takes a shot. "Because every time you two call a truce and then quit speaking, you get all pissy for a month. Maybe longer. You can't handle when the two of you don't get along. Just curious if you're interested in another relapse."

"I don't get pissy," I argue, snagging the ball and dribbling to the top of the court.

"You get pissy," he says, successfully stealing the ball from me.

"No."

"Yes."

"I'm not arguing about this," I say and steal the ball back.

"Okay, but all I'm going to say is either be her friend and keep it that way or date her already."

I laugh but then stop. "What?"

"Oh, come on, you can't be that confused by what I said."

I'm not. It's just that none of my friends have ever said something like this to me before. The whole dating Abby part, I mean.

"Think about it: You two have been best friends since the seventh grade, and then all of a sudden, you start dating and things change, then she starts dating and things change even more, so the only answer is that you two clearly can't see that you want to be together."

I shake my head.

"We're just friends," I tell him.

"Just friends? Maybe you should ask my wife how those situations turn out," he says. But just because this type of situation worked out for him and Sara doesn't mean it'll happen again.

"Abby and I are different. I swear."

"Okay, whatever you say. Just remember this: if you mess it up this time, well, eventually she won't keep giving you more chances. Just friends or not, you could lose her."

He bounces the ball my way, and I fake left.

Lose Abby?

I might do some stupid shit, but she'd never cut me out completely … would she?

CHAPTER SIX

Abby

Meet me behind the ninth-grade bleachers.

I hold the note in my hand as I practically skip my way to that spot. It's been two years since I met Tyler, and we've spent as much of our time together as we can. He's my best friend. Maybe even more than my best friend. Maybe that's why he wants me to meet him behind the bleachers.

Oh my god. What if he kisses me? What do I do? What if I'm a bad kisser? What if ... I hear a girl laughing and my steps freeze.

Who else could randomly be meeting here at this exact moment?

With slow feet, I turn the corner to see Tyler laughing at something on a girl's phone.

"That's so you," she says, pointing to the screen. Tyler's head falls back with a deep laugh, and then he shoves her.

"It is not," he says, and they laugh.

They turn to look at each other; Tyler steps closer to her. Her eyes close and ...

"Hey, Tyler," I call out. I stumble over to them, pretending like I didn't see a thing, and produce the best real smile I can.

"Abs, hey," he says, flashing me the same smile he has since the day we met. "I'm glad you made it," he says to me. "I want you to meet my best friend," he says to the other girl.

Friend.

I swallow.

Friend.

The word plays on repeat as I stare at the brunette with the perfect complexion and clothes my family could never afford. She's got on star dangling earrings, a necklace that matches, and rings on every finger of her right hand. Her makeup looks perfect, and it makes me want to cry. Not because we can't afford makeup, but because she's really pretty and because Tyler is smiling at her like he's never, ever smiled at me.

"Abs, was it?" she asks, and I nod.

"Abby, yeah." I force my grin more and then ask, "What's your name?"

Her smile beams. "I'm Kelsey."

The memory comes back full force when Tyler sends me a text that says, "Meet me by the picnic tables." It's safe to say it's because that's the last time he asked me to meet him somewhere. After that, I always made an excuse not to appear. I wasn't about to go through that heartbreak again.

I park my car near the BA and walk to the park. There have to be at least two hundred people here. I weave my way through the crowd, sneaking peeks at the tables that line the outer sidewalk as I head for the tables.

I spot a dip mix booth that I mentally note to visit before I leave. The picnic tables come into sight and I halt. Kelsey is sitting next to Tyler, laughing at something he said. It's like junior high all over again. Then Ethan approaches the table with their son on his back and their daughter swinging his arm next to him.

I take a deep breath. I'm not in high school anymore, and perhaps Beth is right that Kelsey doesn't hate me anymore.

"Abby, hey!" Kelsey smiles at me and rises. "I didn't know you were coming today. A bunch of us are over at the BA's food truck. The guys are grilling burgers. You should join us."

I swear my heart picks up speed and the temperature turns up a notch. Did Kelsey just invite me to hang out? Is she serious? What do I say? Why can't I move?

"Maybe in a bit. Abs is actually here with me," Tyler says, moving to stand next to me. When his hand snakes behind my back and rests on my hips, only one thing comes to mind: *Oh shit.*

I fully expect Kelsey to say something, but Ethan beats her to it.

"It's about damn time," he says and chuckles. My gaze moves to Kelsey, who is smiling too. Ethan grabs her hand, lifting it to kiss the back before pulling her away.

"Okay, so first, I want you to meet my boss," Tyler says, lacing his hand with mine.

I plant my feet and jerk him back.

"What?" he asks, looking over his shoulder.

I drop his hand and put my hands on my hips. I know my eyes are wide. In fact, I'm giving him the whole what-the-fuck look. He clearly isn't picking up on it.

"What do you mean, what? Tyler, you practically just told Kelsey and Ethan we're a couple by holding me like that in front of them."

Tyler's head tilts as he grins. He pulls my hand back into his. "Because we are."

"But—"

"Abs, from this moment on, to everyone around us, we're together."

Oh no. No. No. No. I thought this was just for his work. Not to everyone. Not to the friends I lost because of what we did. Not to Beth, the one person who still actually hangs out with me. She's going to think I lied to her or kept something or … I don't know. Not dating Tyler for real was my only saving grace that one day we might all be friends again.

"Are you okay?" Tyler asks, dipping his head to meet me at eye level.

"We're lying to a lot more than just your coworkers, Tyler."

His nose wrinkles. "I know, but it's going to be fine."

Tears pinch the backs of my eyes like I'm slicing an onion.

"No, don't do that," Tyler says, wrapping his arms around me.

"But now she'll hate me forever," I manage to say into his now-wrinkled shirt.

"Who? Kelsey?" he asks and pulls away.

I nod.

"Abs, she hasn't been mad for a really long time. Trust me."

"Yeah, but I'll never get her friendship back, and our being together just confirms that—"

"That people change. She's different now. I'm different now. You're definitely different now. If you keep thinking of all the crap that happened in the past, you'll never be able to move forward." He pauses. "Mr. Jinks is headed this way. Do you still want to do this?"

My head jerks back. *He'll still let me out of the deal if it's what I want!*

I processed a lot of things just now, but one thing is for sure: Tyler's right. I'll never be able to move forward if I keep thinking of the past. I don't want to live in the past. I want to live in the now and keep improving. To start, I'm sticking to my word and being the person he needs me to be. After all, being someone that people can trust is who *I* want to be.

"Yes," I say with a deep breath.

"Okay," he says, and I can't help but mirror his grin.

"Mr. Maron." A tall, gray-haired man who reminds me of on an older Pierce Brosnan approaches us with a blonde woman who looks half his age on his arm. "I was beginning to think I wouldn't find you in this crowd," the man goes on.

Tyler chuckles, and my heart immediately warms. It's his real laugh and not a fake one to impress his boss. I wasn't sure what to expect once he was around his coworkers, but it looks like the real Tyler is still here.

"Mr. Jinks, I presume?" I speak up. The man places his hand in mine with a nod. "I've heard wonderful things about your company."

"Thank you. I was beginning to think you were going to say about me, and I was growing curious as to what Tyler could have said," he replies with a chuckle. "This is my wife, Bristle. I'm sorry, I didn't catch your name."

"It's Abby, Abby James."

"Soon be Abby Maron, of course," Tyler cuts in. His soft lips press gently against my temple and places me in a trance that slowly closes my eyes. I know I'm smiling like an idiot. The worst part? I'm not faking how much I'm enjoying the embrace.

"Engaged. I had no idea," Mr. Jinks says loudly enough to draw attention from neighboring booths.

"Oh, please, can I see the ring?" Bristle asks.

My heart sinks, and Tyler's eyes find mine.

Shit.

"It's being resized," he says quickly and tightens his hold on my hand.

I nod. "Yes. That darn thing just kept sliding off. Still," I hold up my left hand. "I feel naked without it already."

"Next time, I suppose," Bristle says.

"Of course."

"These town picnics are always a bore. I don't even know why I come anymore," a voice says behind Tyler's boss, and every hair on my body raises.

Mr. Jinks sighs and steps aside, just as the face that matches the voice comes into view.

Shit. Shit. Shit.

"Tyler, Abby, I'd like you meet my son, Kurt."

I swallow and force a smile as Kurt crosses his arms and widens his stance. If he weren't Tyler's boss's son, I'd slap that smug grin right off his face.

His attention never leaves mine, not even when Tyler says hello and sparks a new subject of conversation. In all honesty, I can't concentrate on this new topic either. It's impossible to focus when the man responsible for sending your mother over the edge is standing right in front of you.

. . .

Tyler

Effortless.

That's how this whole fake relationship with Abby is going. Everyone is really taking a liking to her. If it isn't her shared memories of us growing up, it's her overall presence. Not a single person has excused themselves without implying that we all do something soon. She's a hit, and picking her is proving exactly what I thought: She's perfect.

"And then he jumped off the bleachers, scream-singing *Fly Like a Bird*. He was suspended for two games. I remember it very well because at the following pep rally, everyone tried to petition him back onto the team. It didn't work, of course."

She gazes up at me. Her white smile shines as Sandy and her husband control their laughter.

"I would have never guessed you were so much fun, Tyler. At work, you're very serious," Sandy says.

"Yeah, well, high school was the best years for everyone," I tell her. "That, and I'd rather keep my job than go singing down the halls of the firm with no clothes on."

"Ah, laughter already. I must have missed the punch line of this conversation," Carl says, approaching the four of us. For a moment I was beginning to think he wasn't going to show up, but clearly, I'm not that lucky. I glance over his shoulder to see if anyone is following him, but it seems he's alone.

"You know, I've yet to introduce my husband to everyone, but we should all get together sometime," Sandy says and waves goodbye.

"So, is this the mysterious other half?" Carl asks, and

when he leans forward to speak, the hint of tequila sting my nostrils. Abby's head jerks back and, I slide my hand around her waist and pull her to my side.

"Yes. This is Abby." The lightness that's been in my voice the last couple of hours is gone.

"Abby," he repeats, "I'm Carl," and offers her his hand.

"It's very nice to meet you." She shakes his hand politely but removes it quickly and pats my chest. "Do you mind if I stop by the BA's truck real quick?"

"Not at all," I say and lean forward to kiss her forehead before she turns, leaving me with my least favorite person.

"So, she's real?"

"Of course she's real," I snap back.

"I didn't believe you."

"Clearly."

"But now I see the way you look at her and I can't decide," he says. I wait for him to go on, but he doesn't. Not until I look at him anyway. I couldn't care less what his conflict is.

"I can't decide if it's really love or an act you've perfected."

I grind my teeth as I turn my attention to the little girl sitting at the face-painting booth getting a cat on her left cheek. I'm aware that there are multiple people who want this promotion, but I see now that some are willing to go above and beyond in the wrong way to get it. I'm lying, yes, but I'd never out someone to make myself look better.

"My relationship is none of your business," I say. "Now, excuse me." I move to step around him, but he sidesteps and puts his hand on my chest.

I step back, and I know the look in my eyes shouts *back off.*

"Wind Valley is big but not that big, Maron. If you're lying, it won't take me long to find out."

I don't give him the satisfaction of a reply. My shoulder bumps his as I pass him and head straight for the BA's grill.

"Tyler," Mr. Jinks calls out as he catches up behind me. I pause and take a deep breath. Taking my attitude with Carl out on the boss isn't smart.

"A few of us are gathering at the country club tomorrow at four for nine holes of carefree couples' golf. I'd love it if you and Abby could join us."

"We'd love to." The words spill out before I even think twice whether Abby can make it or not. One extra event should be fine with her, right?

"Wonderful. Unfortunately, my wife won't be joining us, so I'm going to put my son on our team of four."

"That sounds great." Honestly, this short conversation has turned my mood around completely. Being invited to play golf on Mr. Jinks's team has to earn me brownie points of some kind, and then add in getting to know his kid and I'll probably be grinning about this all afternoon.

"Perfect, we'll see you then," he says and heads back to the picnic table where is wife is sitting.

Fuck yes. This is perfect. This is exactly what I wanted. I can't wait to tell Abby.

"Hey, Ethan," I say and glance around the truck. "Where's Abby?"

"Umm." He looks over each shoulder and then to the other side of the truck. "Right there." He points with his spatula.

"Hey, Abs." I pause at her growing laughter. I'd like to say

I stop and focus on how beautiful she is right now, but the man chuckling next to her gains my full attention. Not because I'm mad, but because the way Rob's looking at her.

He needs to cut that bullshit right now.

"It was epic. I couldn't believe it, but, hey, you only go to Brazil once, right?" he says, his gaze meeting mine as I approach. "Tyler," he says with smile. "You better not let this one stray very far." He points to Abby. "I'll see you at the dinner next weekend."

"Yes, of course." Abby beams before giving me her full attention.

"I think he's my favorite so far of all your coworkers," she says, and I hope my face doesn't give away my thoughts.

I don't want him to be her favorite.

"Why?"

She bumps me with her shoulder. "Oh, stop it. Not that like that. I told you, I'm swearing off men, remember? Besides, he was the only person who didn't talk about work. I mean, that Carl guy didn't either, but he was drunk, and I just didn't like the vibe he gave."

You and me both.

"Oh," she adds, "did you know that Rob and his wife are separating?"

What the—? He makes her laugh and he's almost available.

Swearing off men or not, I don't like this.

"No," I say. "I didn't know that. Rob is a lot like me. He likes to keep his personal life separate from work as much as he can."

She nods slowly. The smile sneaking to her lips is contagious.

"What?" I ask.

"Nothing. I just … I actually had fun doing this today."

I sling an arm around her shoulders. "You're telling me. Mr. Jinks is so happy he met you that he's invited us to play a round of golf with him tomorrow."

"I work till two," she says, her lips turning upside down.

"That's all right. We aren't playing till four."

"Oh. Okay."

"It's going to be great. He wants us to be on a team with his son and—"

"You know what," she says cutting me off. "I, um, I actually can't tomorrow."

That's weird.

"You can't?"

"Nope."

"But a second ago you said—"

"Yeah, I just forgot I have plans."

She diverts her gaze from mine, but when I turn her to stand right in front of me, she looks up. She's lying. I know this because she always, *always* reaches for her left ear when she lies.

"What's going on?" I ask.

"Nothing." Another ear grab.

"Abby."

"Tyler."

I sigh. Clearly, I'm not doing too great at this "make her trust me" thing.

"All right," I give in. "You might not want to golf, but I do know something you will want to do," I say and grab her hand, pulling her to follow me.

"What?" She picks up her steps.

"We need to get you a ring, and we need to do it before our next appearance."

"Ooooh," she says, and when I look over my shoulder, her smile is wide.

"I knew you'd like it."

"You know what I else I like?" she asks, and I slow my feet.

"What?"

"Hanging out with you."

I stop completely to look her in the eye.

"Me too."

She moves past me, straight for my truck, looking cute as hell in her blue capris and pink shoulder cut-out top. Something about it reminds me of the days when you could never get the two of us to stop hanging out. I've missed those days. Yet, another part of me, the part in my stomach that's fluttering right now, says … something I can't admit. If I did, it could ruin the friendship I'm starting to get back. I don't want to lose that again.

CHAPTER SEVEN

Abby

Sometimes, I know I should do something, but then I get too nervous, so I chicken out. Well, I wish I had done it now. I wish I had called Beth that day at the park to tell her every-thing. Or to at least give her a heads-up. Right now, yes, a heads-up would have been a good idea.

"What the hell, Abby?" The words are out of Beth's mouth before the door to the BA latches closed.

A few people, both customers and employees, glance my way as my red-headed friend glares at me across the bar. A few of them have curious expressions, but then you have Luke, who is just laughing. No doubt he knows exactly why she's here. This whole Tyler and me thing is receiving more attention than I thought it would.

I smile big at Beth and even wave before turning to find something to do. A quick scan of my tables tells me my work is all caught up, but even if I did have something to do, I would have excused myself anyway, judging from the click of Beth's heels across the floor.

"Break room. Now," she breathes, passing right by me as if she still works here, slamming her hand on the swinging door.

I glance to the bar's entrance. How fast would I have to run? I have flats on and she has heels. I'm no runner, but I bet I could get a pretty good head start.

I let out a deep sigh and drop my chin.

If I run, she'll just follow until she catches me.

I poke my head into the employee's room and find her leaning against the emergency kit counter with her arms crossed. Her whole black skirt, suit, businesswoman ensemble is a bit intimidating. It's like the principal just called me into her office.

"Anything you want to say to me?" she asks.

I shake my head. "Probably nothing you don't already know."

"Abby." She steps toward me.

"Ugh, Beth. It's more complicated than it sounds, and I don't want to get into it," I say quickly, grabbing some rags to look busy.

"Too late. Everyone is talking about it and asking me questions I have zero answers to," she shoots back.

"It's not even that big of a deal, and it's none of their business."

"You're engaged to Tyler and no one even knew the two of you were dating. I'd say it's a big deal."

Another sigh.

I mean, yeah ... when she says it like that, it sounds a bit dramatic.

"That's all you've got?" she asks. "I thought you were trying to change."

Would it be so horrible if I told just one person the truth? I mean, it's Beth. She'd tell me what she thinks with candor and she'll also not tell a soul if I ask her not to. Plus, telling someone might actually help relieve some of the stress, even if it ends up with me disappointing her. She's so eager to see me make changes.

However, it could jeopardize the whole point of why we're doing this and also chance my having to move back into a place where I have to pay rent. Not telling is the way to go.

"I am changing, and yes, that's all I've got because that's the whole story. I'm engaged to Tyler."

I don't wait around for her to say anything. I march right out into the bar, setting the towels I'd gathered on the edge of the bar top and moving on to check on my tables. Her heels tap behind me.

"Are you two doing okay here?" I ask my first table.

They nod and smile.

"Have you set a date?" Beth asks behind me.

"No," I answer as I smile at my next table and clear a dirty plate.

"Are you going to have kids?"

"I don't know," I answer, but there is no stopping my smile.

Kids. With Tyler?

"Summer or winter wedding?"

I shrug. *Summer. Definitely summer.*

"Are you moving in with him, buying a house, getting a new place together or—?"

"Beth," I snap as quietly as I can and move away from hearing distance of any tables.

"What?" she asks. "You're getting married. Aren't these things the two of you have talked about? Most engaged couples know all these answers. The fact that you don't only makes me suspicious of this entire story and … don't roll your eyes at me."

"You sound ridiculous," I say.

"Me? You being engaged to Tyler out of the freaking blue is ridiculous. Are you in trouble? Is that what this is? Because I swear to God, if that boy—"

I grab her wrist and pull her back into the employee's room. She's not going to let up until I give her something more, and I know I said no, but, this is Beth. She's the one friend who's been here for me through all my mess-ups.

"Okay, okay. Calm down," I say.

She pins me with a glare.

"Well, while yes, if …" Shoot, I'm saying this all wrong. "Tyler needed a fake fiancée to get this promotion at work and so he asked me, and that's why I moved into his rental because that was part of the deal, and so for the next few weeks I'm the future Mrs. Maron, and although we're lying to everyone, I … it's going to be fine."

She presses her lips together, unfolding her arms and resting her hands on her hips. Her mouth opens but nothing comes out.

"Crazy, huh?" I force a smile.

She nods once, her focus on the floor. "Abby, you know I've never held back on letting you know when you have a stupid idea, which is most of the time—"

"Hey," I cut in. "Not all of the time."

"Well, do you really think this is smart?"

I study the shelf of paper towels behind her as if the Brawny man is going to change my answer. No. It's definitely not smart, but I needed a new place to live. I didn't see any other option that still allowed my mom stay in rehab.

"It's going to be fine, but swear you won't tell anyone," I say.

Her brows hit the middle of her forehead. "If I can't tell anyone, that's a giant red flag you shouldn't be doing it."

"Well, it's a good thing it doesn't affect you, isn't it?"

"Abby, I'm not trying to be mean, but it's no secret you have feelings for Tyler even if he's the only person who can't see it."

"Stop saying my name like I'm some kid you can't get to pay attention, all right? I don't have feelings for Tyler," I say. "Anymore."

Her hips pop to the right.

"I don't," I repeat.

"Sure. What kind of job needs you to have a fiancée to get a promotion?" Her face scrunches up.

"I think it's more for the look of stability and this whole 'it's all about family' thing they have going on."

"It sounds stupid. What happens when he gets the promotion? You just mysteriously break up?" she asks.

If you ever want to know what it feels like to have your heart drop to your stomach … stop wondering. It sucks. She may as well have just told me I have to move back into my old apartment and live there for the rest of my life.

We never came up with a plan for when it is all said and done. I'd assume we'd just … I don't know … have a calm, mutual breakup and then stay friends.

"Just promise you won't tell anyone," I say again. I don't want to think about after. Beth is my friend—I'd tell her that I need this more than he needs me, but that leads to more questions of why and more questions I don't want to answer.

"I won't, but this is a bad idea. Makes more sense now, but still, not a good idea."

"Look, I just … I wanted to do something for someone else for once. He needed a favor and it was something I could do. I'm trying to be a better person, Beth."

Beth lets out a long breath. "You can be a better person without getting your heart broken," she says.

"I won't."

She nods slowly. "I'll repeat that this is a horrible, *horrible* idea, but, that said, if you need anything, you know where to find me."

She gives me a quick hug. "I've got to get back to work."

"All right."

"Abby, I'm serious. If you need me, I'm here."

"Thank you."

The door swings closed with her absence. I let out a long breath and sit on a stack of boxes.

What happens when he gets the promotion?

Will I just go back to living a life where I struggle to pay my bills while he gets everything he wants?

I mean, I'm getting what I want right now. I'm getting all of Tyler's attention, even if it is fake. It only makes sense he gets what he wants in the end.

Shit.

Beth's right.

I should *not* pretend to date the guy I've wanted to be with since seventh grade. It's a bad idea, but it's too late. I'm in it now.

Tyler

My clubs rattle behind me as I make my way down the hill. Golfing with the boss. If that doesn't say I'm looking good for the promotion, then the fact I'm on his team definitely does.

Mr. Jinks and his son are standing at the end of the first row of parked carts. I'm stoked we're taking a cart, but I would walk all day long if that's what Mr. Jinks wanted.

Kiss-ass? Determined is what I call it.

"Tyler, so glad you could make it," Mr. Jinks calls out when he sees me.

Kurt is sitting the cart, leaning back with his ankles crossed over the dash. He's got a smug grin on his face as he watches me. What the hell? I've only met him once.

"Morning," I say and drop my bag off my shoulder.

"While you get your bag situated, I'm going to run into the pro shop real quick," Mr. Jinks says and heads back up the hill.

I'm almost finished strapping my bag into my cart when Kurt asks, "Where's your fiancée?" The way he says *fiancée* makes my skin crawl. I'm glad she had other plans.

"She had another commitment," I say.

"Doing what?"

I side-eye him and then focus on my golf bag, pretending to look for something in the right pocket. I have no idea what she's doing. Should I have asked?

"She's just out with some of her friends."

"Friends? Does she even have those?" he asks, and my attention jerks to him. Why does he say it like he knows her?

"Yes. She has friends."

"You're positive."

The look in his eyes is insinuating. He knows something I don't. My hand clenches as I step toward him.

"Finally. I'm sorry, boys. I just wanted to use my new driver, and the gentleman in shop was having a hard time finding it," Mr. Jinks says. "Are we good to go?"

Kurt keeps his gaze on me, waiting for my answer.

I nod. "Yeah, Mr. Jinks, we're good."

"Ah, call me Marshall. Out here I like to be relaxed, and Mr. Jinks is too damn formal for my day off."

"Sounds good to me, and, yes, I think we're all set." I hop in my cart.

"I'm here, I'm here!" a voice shouts, causing us all to turn. Really though, he causes a lot of people to turn to look at him. Yelling at the golf course isn't exactly applauded.

"Carl," Marshall says. "I thought you said you couldn't make it."

"Ahh, well," he says and looks my way. "Figured this would be a great game, what with all the stories I've heard at how good your swing is. I didn't want to miss it."

That. That is a kiss-ass.

"Great" is all Marshall says, and I try not to laugh.

Marshall and Kurt pull away while I wait for Carl to load his bag.

"You didn't think I would let you have this moment all to yourself, did you?" he asks. I keep my attention on the cart dash, confirming there is a scorecard and pencil ready to go.

"No answer? I'm going to guess that means you thought you did."

Carl drops himself into the seat next to me and grins. "You're not the best, Maron. It's time you realize it."

If I slammed my fist into his face before we even reach the first tee box … would I lose my job?

Probably.

Damn it.

* * *

"I had no idea you play that well, Maron," Marshall says as we take our seat around an outside table that overlooks the ninth hole. We're the only table out here, and my guess is that Marshall is trying to keep us as far away from other members as he can. Carl still hasn't picked up on the whole "being a bit quieter at the golf course" thing.

"Lucky day is what I'd call it," Carl says. He shoots me a smug grin, but then notices our boss watching him. "Maybe next time you can rub some of that luck off on me. I could use a swing like yours."

To anyone else, it was a kind compliment; I heard every ounce of pain it took for him to say something nice.

"We could all use a swing like Tyler's," Marshall adds. The waitress comes up and steals his attention. Carl takes this moment to lean in toward me.

"I don't know what game you're playing, but it's not going to last," he says.

I focus on the menu. A BLTA sounds good, but so does the French dip.

"No comment, eh? Figures. You were never one to fight for what you want. I mean, I—"

"Don't know when to shut up," I finish the sentence for him. "You don't like me. I get it. I also don't care. I fight when it's necessary, and arguing with you over whose damn golf game is better is a waste of time."

"You're just—"

"Shall we order?" Marshall asks.

I nod, and so do Kurt and Carl.

Once our orders are placed, Kurt excuses himself from the table.

"How are sales going these past two weeks?" Marshall asks.

"Great. I've got a bid pending on a couple houses," Carl speaks up.

"Good, good, and you, Tyler?"

"I didn't see any new bids placed for him since the Wolcott house," Carl offers.

"That's correct. I didn't have any bids last week. I did, however, close on two houses."

"That's magnificent." Marshall beams. "You two are going places, and I am thrilled to have you on my team. How would the two of you feel about giving a joint presentation on effective selling approaches to the others one afternoon? I'd love to see them learn something from the both of you."

Team up with Carl? Real answer? Fuck no. Work answer: Sure, when?

"Our selling practices are very different," Carl says.

"True, but I think if we put them together, we could really bring something to the group" is my reply.

"I couldn't agree more," Marshall says.

Our food arrives, and Kurt still hasn't returned from the bathroom.

"Should we wait?" I ask.

"No, he should be back any moment," Marshall says. It sounds rehearsed. Almost as if he knew someone was going to ask.

Carl digs right into his food.

"I'm going to go wash up," I say. Marshall's hand freezes with a fork full of food halfway to his mouth. He doesn't look my way; he just nods.

Kurt is the first thing I see when I push open the door to the men's locker room. He's sitting in a chair that's facing away from me, leaned back, and on his phone.

"I shit you not, they're engaged. I'm telling you, something doesn't add up. A few months ago, she wasn't with a single person and now—" Kurt stops mid-sentence and looks back over the chair. His gaze collides with mine. "I've got to go. We'll finish this later."

His rises slowly, never breaking our eye contact.

"Do you always listen in on other people conversations?" he asks.

"Not intentionally," I say with a grin. Two things I know for sure right now: He was definitely talking about Abby, and he is not a fan of people overhearing him. If his shaking hand doesn't give that away, it is the uncertainty in his eyes. "Although, I am curious why you'd be sitting in a men's bathroom talking on your phone about my fiancée."

He finally breaks eye contact and smiles wide. "I guess if you wanted to know the answer, you should have walked in sooner."

He moves to step past me, but I reach a hand out to stop

him. "You'd be smart to never talk about my fiancée again. In fact, it'd be smart if you just forget about her completely."

He laughs.

"If you actually knew who your fiancée is, I'm not so sure you'd be standing up for her."

He tries to move again, but I hold him in his place.

"I know who she is. I also know that if we have another conversation about her, you'll have wished you listened the first time."

He shakes his head, making a *tsk* noise. "Threatening the boss's son. That's a ballsy move to make."

Shit. That hadn't even occurred to me.

"I'll tell you what. Next time I want to talk about her, I'll come to you first and then we can decide what we want to do. After all, we all have secrets that we don't want others to know, right?"

He waits for my answer, but I don't have one. I threatened my boss's son. That's all I can think about. This is definitely not the way to get the promotion. If I keep this up, it's a no for sure. The best thing I can do is forget this happened and move on.

CHAPTER EIGHT

Abby

I never knew my stomach could growl so loudly. Shoot, it's like a dog ready to attack an intruder. Except I'm not about to fight; I'm ready to freaking eat. Obviously, I haven't eaten all day, and it's not because I haven't wanted to, but because of where I'm headed and who I could run into.

Had I known Kurt would be around, there is a good chance I would have said no to Tyler's offer. What will I do if he tells his dad and his dad says something to Tyler? Or what if he says something about our connection in front of all these people?

At the picnic, I'd met people who didn't know anything about me. They met the new Abby. The Abby I'm focusing on, and if Kurt comes up and starts talking … I don't think I could handle it.

"Are you cold?" Tyler asks. "You're covered in goose bumps."

I shake my head and force a smile.

I wish it were the temperature.

Tyler squeezes my hand as we make our way around the right side of his boss's house. It's a gorgeous white brick home full of windows, and from the looks of it, each bedroom has its own balcony. Two parts of the house have points that remind me of a castle. The landscaping is to die for. It even has a waterfall with goldfish in the small pond that lines the driveway as you pull up toward the front doors. The house is circled by pine trees, giving the backyard, where the dinner is being held, all the privacy you could need. The surrounding flowers give it the perfect outdoor smell and color that make you want to visit a greenhouse on the way home just to recreate the look.

"This place is insane," Tyler whispers.

"Yes, it is," I whisper back. I don't know why we whisper; the place is too flipping big for anyone to hear us anyway.

We both laugh.

"I feel underdressed," I tell him and glance down at my pale blue summer dress and strappy white sandals. Yep, even in a dress I still feel underdressed.

"You look beautiful," he replies with another squeeze of his hand.

As we near what I assume is the edge of the house and the beginning of the backyard, voices grow louder. As expected, the yard is filled with guests. However, it's the shining red hair in the corner that catches my eye.

"What is Beth doing here?" I ask.

Shit.

Super shit.

Is she spying on me?

"She didn't tell you she was coming? The company she

works for is one of the few who do our advertising," Tyler says.

"Oh, I didn't realize this event would have more people than just those you work with." Hopefully, he can't tell from my voice that I am worried.

"Yeah, I'm afraid we never know who to expect," he says as we glance around, not exactly sure in which direction to head first.

Oh, that's fantastic.

"Tyler, Abby, hey," Sandy says as she spots us. "We saved you a place at our table. Your friends are sitting with us too." She points toward Beth, who is now waving at us.

"That's wonderful. Thanks, Sandy," Tyler says. "Which way to the drink table?"

"I'll show you," she offers.

"Do you want anything?" Tyler asks me.

"Just a water is fine. I'm going to say hi to Beth."

He kisses me on the cheek.

I know I blush when he does this, but I can't help it. Fake or not, I enjoy the way it makes me feel.

Wanted.

Secure.

Happy.

I smile, waving at a few people I'd met at the picnic last week as I cross the lawn.

"Well, well, well, look at you two walking in holding hands," Beth says in greeting.

My eyes widen, and I glance at Beth's fiancé—real fiancé—Maverick.

"Like I wouldn't tell him. The fiancé never counts when there is a secret involved," she says with a grin.

"Ugh." I sigh and drop my face into my hands.

"I've got to admit," Maverick begins, "I'm normally one for happy endings, but from what Beth tells me, you two are creating quite the mess of lies."

"Shhh," I say, and there is a chance I may have stomped my foot a little as I glance around the yard. It's pointless though; the space is so damn big, everyone is pretty well spaced out.

"What Tyler and I decided to do is our business, okay? Let's change the topic."

Maverick chuckles. "You two chat. I'm going to go find Tyler."

"He's getting drinks," I tell him.

"Awesome. Thanks."

Beth doesn't wait long.

"So, how's it really going?" she asks.

"Fine. We've only been to one function other than this one," I say.

"I heard. So, tell me about this 'ring' you are having sized."

I hold up my left hand to show her the teardrop ring. Knowing Beth, she spotted it as a knockoff from Target ASAP.

Her eyes meet mine.

"Of all the rings, you pick this one?"

"Hey, I like this one."

"Okay …" she says, but there is small smile touching her lips. "So, not to make things weird, but in the, say, five minutes, give or take, that you've been standing here, you've gained an admirer."

She looks over my shoulder, nodding for me to look.

My stomach drops.

I turn back around and close my eyes. I didn't see him. No. He's not here.

"Do you know him?" Beth asks.

I nod.

"Is he an ex?"

"Oh, god no," I say and look back.

Kurt's gone now.

"Why are you so shiny?" Beth asks.

I shake my head.

"He dated my mom," I tell her.

Please don't come back.

"Seriously?" The single-word question comes out with a squeak.

"Yes."

"How old is he? Like twenty years her junior?"

"Pretty close. My mom has sort of lost control these days."

And that's as much as I will share about her.

"I'll say," Beth adds. "I'll go tell him to cut the crap."

"No." I quickly grab her arm. "You can't. He's Tyler's boss's kid."

"What?"

"Yeah, talk about awkward."

Awkward.

Awful.

Same thing.

"I'm guessing no one knows about him and your mom."

"Nope."

"Not even Tyler?" she asks.

I shake my head.

"Damn. That's an intense secret to keep," she adds.

Not as intense as the fact my mom used to deliver drugs for him until I called the cops on her and had her arrested. Hence, why she's in rehab.

"Yeah. Intense."

"Is it smart not to share this piece of information with Tyler?"

I shrug. "I haven't decided yet."

"What are you two talking about?" Tyler asks behind me.

I turn, and Tyler chooses that exact moment to lean in for a cheek kiss. Except my movement lands the kiss at the corner of my lips.

I should jump back.

He should jump back.

Neither of us moves.

When Tyler pulls away, his eyes find mine.

I wish I could read what they are saying, but I can't.

"So, you two are cute," Beth says, and Maverick nudges her hip. "Jeez, what? It was a compliment."

"Well, it's easy when you have a fiancée who looks like Abby," Tyler says, and cliché as it is, my heart melts. Could you image how I'd act if this were real?

Dang it. Abby, no! Friends. Just friends.

"Yeah …" is all Beth says.

"Tyler!" All four of us turn our attention to the voice.

Rob is headed this way, and I'll admit, his smile is extra welcoming.

"Do you mind if I pick your brain really quick on a sales question? I have a buyer who wants to look at a house first thing in the morning, and since you sell more houses than the rest of us, why not consult you beforehand, right?" Rob points out.

"Sure," Tyler answers.

"Perfect. Hey, Abby, how are you?"

"I'm doing good, and yourself?"

"This isn't Brazil, but I guess I'll take it," he says, his arms opening as he spins to look around the greenery.

I laugh.

"Let's walk and talk," Tyler says, his gaze colliding with mine before he shoos Rob away from the group.

I roll my eyes as I twist to face Beth and Maverick.

"What?" I ask at Beth's big eyes.

"What do you mean what? Did you see Tyler just now?"

"Yes … he is always like that when Rob's around. It's normal."

"Ha. Tyler being jealous of you and another man is normal? Damn, maybe you were right." She looks at Maverick. "Maybe they will hit it off."

"You think?" I ask.

"I knew it!" Beth shouts. "You are not just friends."

"Yes, we are."

"On the outside maybe, but you still want more."

"Beth, stop."

"Hey, you're the one who just had a hopeful look on her face and tried lying to me."

"So what, so what if I like him? I've always liked him, and nothing has ever come of it and nothing ever will come of it. End of story."

A drunken almost night doesn't count.

"I still don't like it."

"Yes, I know," I say and notice Maverick just grinning.

"What?" I ask.

"I like when someone can dish it back to her," he says with a laugh. "It's fun to watch when you're not a part of it."

This makes me laugh too. Beth looks ready to break, but then she smiles and kisses her fiancé.

Normally, I'm not bothered by this kind of thing, but right now, watching this simple interaction between them, I want it. I want more. And there is only one person I want more with.

Tyler

Boring.

Aside from Rob, no one at this barbeque has mentioned a word about work. Which is great, but when you are in a group gathering with people who are coworkers and not friends, what do you talk about?

Work.

So, basically, besides my table, the whole gathering is fairly quiet.

"Dude, I'm telling you. He touched the rim," Maverick says.

He's been trying to convince me that Logan dunked the ball at the gym. I was just there with Logan the other week and he missed at least fifty percent of his shots.

"And I'm telling you, there is no way that's possible. Abby, what do you think?" I ask.

She sips her drink. "I think Logan is married to my boss and he dunked it," she says.

Both of my hands shoot up. "Ah, that doesn't count," I tell her.

"It counts," Maverick adds.

"I'm with Tyler," Beth says, and I high-five her across the table.

"Thank you."

"How is it not possible?" Maverick shakes his head. "He goes to the gym almost every day. It was bound to happen."

"I watched him play in junior high, and let's just say he wasn't on the A or B team." Beth laughs.

Maverick rolls his eyes at her and then starts to pinch at her sides while she pretends to be mad about it.

"Fine," I say, interrupting them. "If he's done it once, he'll do it again, right? A hundred bucks says the next time we shoot hoops, he can't do it," I say.

"Deal." Maverick and I shake on it.

"Why does it matter?" Abby asks.

I shrug. Maverick shrugs. "Just does."

"Okay, well this has been great, but we should be going," Beth says, and Maverick nods.

"The future Mrs. is right," he adds. His gaze slowly turns to mine. "You might want to remember that."

I roll my eyes and can still hear him and Beth laughing as they walk away.

"Do you want to head out?" I ask Abby.

"Sure."

Sandy and her husband left about a half hour ago, along with a few others, so thankfully we aren't the first awkward group to leave.

We say good-bye to Marshall and Bristle and, funny enough, both Abby and I sigh when we get in the truck.

"What's your sigh for?" I ask.

"Because I ate too much." She answers without missing a beat. "You?"

"Because I didn't want to have to make small talk with any other coworkers."

"Yeah, I swear that one lady, I think she said she is the receptionist, was going to bore you to death. Do you even remember what she was talking about? You were staring at the flowerbed behind her like a body was about to crawl out."

I nod. "Yeah, because how can one person go on about their fish like that? A dog, maybe, but her fish … no."

"Oh, and thank goodness that Carl guy didn't show up," Abby adds.

I nod and start my truck. "Yeah, I was pretty pleased with that myself."

"I get the feeling people at your work don't care for him," she says. "The only person who hinted she wanted him here was that Macy gal."

"You want to hear a secret?" I ask and bounce my eyebrows at her.

She nods quickly.

"I once caught Carl and Macy making out in his office. They don't know I saw them."

"What! Office sex. No way."

"Ew, gross." I cringe. "I just saw them kissing."

"Well, you don't know if they did more," she says.

"I don't want to know if they did more."

"What else have you got for me?" Abby asks as she slouches back in the passenger's seat, crossing one leg over the other as she looks out the window.

I've missed this. Her. Just hanging out and talking about anything that comes to mind.

When we were in junior high, my mom swore we were

going to get married, but then I met Kelsey and we started high school and things … changed. Abby and I changed.

"Huh?" she asks, looking over at me. "Do you have more gossip?"

"Nope, not unless you count the fact that I think my boss's son is a drug dealer as gossip."

Instead of the carefree laughter I got from the first shared secret, Abby's smile drops, and a blank look comes over her face.

"I'm kidding," I say quickly. Damn, I didn't expect her to look so freaked out. "It was a joke."

"Oh, ha. Good one."

Clearly.

I pull into the driveway of Abby's rental and put the truck in park.

"I had fun tonight," she says, and her beautiful grin is back.

"So did I."

I lean over to give her a hug just as she asks, "Do you want to come inside?"

Normally, when a woman asks me this, I'm jumping all over the chance to say yes. But this is Abby. *Abs.* The best friend I lost and am finally getting back. The girl who, no matter how hard I try these days, I can't seem to just look at as a friend.

"I didn't mean for that to sound so … flirtatious."

"Flirtatious?" I repeat.

She punches my shoulder. "You know what I mean. Tonight was fun, and it reminded me of how much I like hanging out with you, so I just thought that since it's only eight, we could, I don't know, keep hanging out."

I tap the wheel and then shut off the ignition.

"That's a brilliant idea."

"Yeah, cool," she says and hops out of the truck.

Abby's smell, like cucumber and mint, surrounds me the moment I step inside.

"Do you want a water or a soda? I don't have beer," she says, heading for the kitchen.

"Water is good."

I plop myself onto her couch, shuck off my shoes, and prop my feet on the ottoman as I turn on the TV.

"Hey, *The Office* is on!" I shout.

"What! No way." She practically runs back into the living room. "God, I'm pretty sure we watched every single episode together for at least the first six seasons."

"Religiously. We never missed a night," I add.

Abby takes the spot next to me, curling her knees into her body and letting them fall against my legs. Without thinking, I rest my hands on her bare skin. She stiffens, and that's when I realize my hand is on her thigh and my pinky finger has snuck its way under the hem of her dress.

I should move my hand. But just as earlier tonight when I should have pulled away when I practically kissed her, I don't pull away now. I turn my gaze to hers.

I swallow, and her gaze drops to my mouth.

Fuck, my heart has never raced this fast before in my life. I've never wanted to kiss someone so badly. I've never wanted to go so caveman and crawl on top of her and do whatever she asks me to as I run my hands over every inch of her. My hands shake against her legs and then a crazed commercial comes on where some guy is screaming, and the simple distraction removes the heat building between us.

We don't say much for the rest of the night; we just watch TV and laugh till it hurts, as if we've never seen a single episode before. I don't know about her, but I finished all the seasons when it first ran. When the last season aired, I'd wanted to call her but didn't. I should have. I should have called so many times.

After a good six episodes, and with more reruns on the schedule lineup, Abby shifts on the couch. Her body sinks into mine, her head resting against me. I adjust myself to get comfortable and … she's asleep.

I stare at her longer than I should. For the past few years, I've lived the single life and focused on my career. I've been happy. I've never felt like anything was missing, but right now, watching Abby sleep, it's different. This right here, it makes me feel like I've been missing something.

And I was.

Not just my best friend, but her.

Abby.

All of her.

My heart beats so loudly, I swear it will wake her.

I pull the blanket over her shoulders. It covers a little of me too. Then I turn off the TV and rest my head on the back of the couch.

God, I've missed you, Abs.

Damn it.

Don't let your feelings ruin this, Tyler. You just got your best friend back.

CHAPTER NINE

Abby

My heart pounds and my hands shake. The way they always do when I get here.

The parking lot at the rehab center is full, so I drive the space twice before I catch the reverse lights of a white Toyota 4Runner in the back row.

This isn't the first time I've shown up and the lot was full, and I know it sounds crazy, but sometimes I want to convince myself it's a sign that I'm not supposed to be here. The only reason my mother is here is because of me. It was this or jail. She chose rehab because I told her I'd pay for it. Some days, I'm pretty sure she picked this just to punish me. I don't think she actually wants to get better.

"Hi, Abby," Mason, my mother's lead nurse, grins at me as the doors slide open. Mason is just under six feet tall, but when he stands behind the reception desk, he looks closer to seven. His black hair is buzzed short like always, and his blue eyes shine as they watch me approach.

"Hi, Mason. How is she today?" I ask.

His lips form a firm line and he looks away. "Today isn't her best day." He drops into the chair behind him.

A gentle smile touches his lips and he looks up at me; this look right here is exactly why I've never told a single person about my mother.

"I'd never tell you not to see your mother, but maybe another day is better," he says softly.

A nurse in periwinkle-blue scrubs with a bun on her head and one arm pinning a clipboard against her chest waves at Mason. He smiles back at her, but then his gaze meets mine and his smile vanishes.

The faint sound of bad elevator music plays around us as he waits for me to say something. I have left a handful of times without seeing her, but maybe today will be different and I'll be glad I stayed.

"Thanks for the heads up," I tell him and knock on the counter as I walk off.

I've always been afraid of hospitals, and although this isn't one, the silence the hallway carries provides the same vibe. When I first researched centers for my mom, I'd thought they would be like the ones on TV, that she'd be out doing yoga or other spiritual stuff and mingling with other patients, but I was wrong. She could do that stuff if she wanted, but it's my mother and she thinks everyone is the enemy. She leaves her room only to eat and attend her required meetings.

Since her room is at the end of the hall, I have to pass quite a few residents on the way. I know it's Mr. Parkins who coughs to my left, that Mrs. Martin in the room next to him will be sleeping right now, and Alice, the woman who is only a few years older than me, is the voice I hear to my left reading to her son.

I don't know why any of them are here; that's not the point. The point is, they are here and trying because they want to be a part of their families again.

It's something I can only wish my mother would want.

Her door is open. Still, I knock before I go inside. Eyes that look exactly like mine glance to the door. Her gaze pauses, but then she returns her focus to the rerun of *Wings* in front of her.

"Hi, Mom," I say and take the seat next to her. "Which episode are we on today?"

I know she won't answer, but still, I show up here every other week to see her.

We sit in silence until the episode is over. Her cheeks look fuller, her arms no longer display evidence of her scratching, and her leg no longer bounces when she sits still. Little things, but all big steps.

I'll save my display of happiness until I leave, though. She may not speak to me, but she does throw things when she's extra mad.

"I moved into a new place," I tell her. "It's much nicer than the one I was in, and the best part is, I don't have to pay rent, which mean you can stay here the full term and I'll still …"

She turns the volume on the TV up a notch.

I swallow and look toward the door. My gaze meets Mason's as he leans against the wall, watching me. He's got a box of Kleenex in his hand.

"I'll see you next time, okay, Mom?"

Standing, I squeeze her hand, but she jerks it away.

I leave before she can see the tears.

I grab a Kleenex from Mason and say a quick thank you as I leave.

The sun is warm against my skin and helps to dry the tears I've let out.

She's my mother. She'll always be my mother and I'll never stop being there for her no matter how she treats me. She'll figure it out one day. She has to. I need her to. I need my mother. What girl doesn't?

* * *

His voice is low, and when he leans in, I can feel the warmth of his breath on my ear.

"Every kiss. Every touch. Every stroke should make you moan, Abby. You should feel it all the way to your toes each time we connect, and I have a pretty damn good feeling I'm the only guy who has ever made you feel that way."

"No," I say. But I know he's right. I know he knows how crazy he makes me. God, just him being this close to me right now makes my stomach spin.

He reaches up a hand to stop the shake and then his lips come so close to mine that if I even flinch, we'll kiss. His other hand runs up my arms, and he's right again. I feel it. The simple touch creates an ache between my legs that I could never admit to him exists.

I jerk up, my sheets slipping down my body. My phone is ringing.

Holy crap.

This is bad.

This is so, *so* bad.

I take a deep breath and move for the bathroom.

Cold water on my face removes the sheen I acquired from my dream.

I can't be having sex dreams about Tyler. I can't. It's not good. I mean, it's good. God, was it good, but I can't. It's so wrong. It'll ruin everything.

New rule: Tyler can no longer fall asleep on my couch. It's been four days since I woke up, snuggled into his side, and my mind clearly can't let it go.

I scrub the makeup off my face that I'd put on before I went to visit my mom. I'd only meant to take quick nap after seeing her.

I'm just two events in and the more time I spend with Tyler, the faster everything I've ever felt for him comes flooding back.

Ugh.

I breathe slowly.

I just need to get a hold of myself. He hasn't noticed. He won't notice. Everything will be just fine.

I let out a long breath and sit, flinching when the back of my legs touch the porcelain toilet.

I have a mother for whom I'd do anything to show her how much I love her, and I have Tyler, for whom I'd do anything to make sure he didn't find out how much I did. How screwed up is my life right now?

Being an adult and not screaming out every emotion is hard.

The *Friends* theme song ringtone I set for Tyler goes off once more. I stare at his name, pulling myself together before I answer.

"Hey, Tyler," I say, and cringe at my overly cheerful

voice.

"Hey, I'm at your door. Do you want to let me in?" he says with a laugh.

My knees pop as I jerk my body into stand. Then I catch my pinky toe on the doorframe.

"Holy mother of … ahh!"

"What is it?" Tyler asks, and the front doorknob jiggles.

"Why are you here?" I ask even though I'd rather shout out a string of swear words. Is my pinky toe still there?

Yes. Okay. Good.

"Is that why you're cursing? Because I'm at your place?"

"No, and I'm not cursing."

"Are you going to let me in?"

"Shit."

"You're cursing now." He laughs, and his smile is the first thing to grab my attention when I swing the door open. That, and the way his tank top clings to his body.

Holy. Shit.

"Did you run here?" I ask, but he doesn't answer me. His eyes are wide and looking everywhere but at mine.

"Tyler?"

"Damnit, Abs!" he shouts and turns around. "Do you always answer the door like this?"

"Like what?" I laugh, my own gaze looking down to my clothes.

I gasp.

Or no clothes.

"I …" I have no idea what I was about to say. "I'll go put some shorts on" is what finally comes out.

"That would be good," he says.

I spin for my room and hear Tyler curse. I yank on some

red yoga pants and then return to the door only to find him sitting on my couch with his face in his hands.

"What's wrong?" I sit next to him. His rises slightly and moves away.

Okay then. Is this because he saw me in my underwear?

"Nothing. Nothing. I'm fine."

"If you say so."

It's definitely got to be the underwear.

"I did."

"All right," I say, pinching my lips to hold in my laughter. Why is he acting so weird? "I assume you came over for a reason other than to sit on my couch, refusing to look at me."

At this, his gaze snaps to mine. "I'm not avoiding you."

I smile.

He rolls his eyes and stands. "I did come here for a reason, and that reason is because this weekend, my boss wants to take a select few of us to some lake resort in Colorado for the weekend."

"What?"

Nope. Nope. Nope. I cannot go away with Tyler.

"A whole weekend, Tyler. It's the Fourth of July," I say. If I make this about work, he won't know it's because going out of town with the guy I was just sex dreaming about is a bad idea.

Bad.

"Yes, and I know you have other things to do, but I need you to come with me. I can't go without you."

My heart softens, but then I remember he doesn't want me there because he's attracted to me—it's because we have a deal.

"I never told you there would be a weekend getaway, so if

you say no, I'll still hold up my end of the deal and we can continue when I get back, but, Abs, there will be boating and jet skis and sun and water, and I don't know about you, but a weekend of fun doesn't sound half bad."

He flashes me a grin, and I'm about to say no again when my eyes fall to my mother's next bill on the coffee table.

I'd almost had a panic attack when Tyler spotted it the other day. He'd be the last person to judge me about my mother, but, da— … dang it, I don't want to be the girl who still has a drug addict mother. I don't want to see his gaze soften or his lips droop when he hears I'm still hoping one day she'll figure her life out. It's embarrassing and exhausting.

A weekend away might not be such a bad idea. I could use the break. Once, just once, I want to walk in there and have her at least look at me. Have her see everything I've done for her. How hard I've worked to help her.

This quick trip could be the distraction I need.

"Friday through Sunday?"

"Yes." His smile grows.

I move toward the kitchen and touch my lips to hide my smile from him. Once I've got it under control, I face him again and shrug. "Sure, why not?"

"Yes," he cheers, his fist jabbing the air above him. "This is going to be great. I'll pick you up around lunch on Friday."

"Okay."

There is bounce to his step as he heads for the door. "Oh, Abs."

"Yeah?"

"We have to share a room," he says and closes the door behind him before I can respond.

Yeah, I'm officially in way over my head.

Tyler

Abby's naked ass is all I can think about.

Which isn't good. At all. Especially now that I'm sitting outside her apartment, waiting for her so we can go out of town for the weekend together.

This is bad.

She appears in the front door with a smile that I really, *really* shouldn't enjoy the way I am. Her backpack gets stuck and the black bag hanging off her right shoulder drops to the brick pathway.

Jogging up to help her, I grab her bag and then open the door wider.

"Thanks," she says with a laugh. "I wasn't sure what to bring, so I'm pretty sure I overpacked."

"How can you overpack? All you need is a pair of shorts and a swimsuit."

She pauses behind me.

"What?" I ask over my shoulder.

"You are such a guy," she says and walks past me.

"Well, we're only going to the lake. It's not like you'll be wearing … you know what, you're right," I concede to avoid finishing the thought of her not wearing much in the way of clothing all weekend.

Which, fuck, I thought anyway.

"You're being weird again. Are you going to be this way all weekend?" she asks.

I toss her bags into the back of the truck with my own and

make a face that probably says I'm being even more weird but that I'm hoping says, "No, definitely not."

"Oh, this is going to be fun," she says and climbs in the truck.

I left my engine running, so once I'm buckled, I pull onto the road. I reach for the radio, but Abby turns it off.

"Can I ask you something?"

"Sure," I say and focus on the road.

"Are you being weird because you saw me in my panties yesterday?"

"What?" The truck swerves a little when I look at her.

"Watch the road," she says, a small smile touching her lips. Her tongue sneaks out, leaving them with a glazed coat, and now all I can think about is how I want my tongue to do that for her.

Shit.

"Well?" she prompts me.

"No, that's not why." I shake my head. I need to change this subject.

"But you agree you're being weird?"

"I guess. Maybe I'm nervous."

"About me?"

Fuck if I know anymore.

"No, about this job and everything we're doing. Let's change the topic," I say. I'm just making shit up now, and the last thing I want is to have a bunch of lies between us.

"All righty then, what do you want to talk about? Since we are sharing a room, maybe we should make some rules."

"You and your rules," I say with a chuckle, but, yeah, she's probably right. Ground rules would be good. Such as, she sleeps in her bed and I'll sleep in mine and we don't touch or undress in front of each other.

"Well, we need to keep this as believable as possible. So which side of the bed do I sleep on?" she asks.

Again, I laugh. "They won't care." Although, if I had to answer, I'd say it doesn't matter as long as she curled up with me.

Wait.

Shit.

Come one, Maron, you can't do this now.

"You don't know the type of stuff that could come up. I just like to be prepared and—oh yes, I love this," she says, turning the volume up to play the new Halsey song. Her soft voice fills the cab of my truck as she sings along, and I can't seem to pull my gaze off of her as she rests her head on the window, gazing out at the open landscape around us. I focus on her lips and then on the twitch of her nose when she gets to a pitch she can't quite hit, but I still can't help but smile.

I can't fall for her.

It's not part of the plan.

Don't mess this up.

She's only helping me out.

Don't take advantage of it.

She's my friend.

She adjusts herself to get comfortable and I catch the moment her shorts inch up her thighs, barely covering her ass.

I look back to the road and grip the steering wheel.

I am so totally and completely fucked.

The afternoon sun streams in through the windows, heating the truck and glaring right into Abby's eyes, waking her from the nap she's been in since we crossed the border between Wyoming and Colorado.

She rights herself, and when she turns to smile at me, it's interrupted by a yawn. "I'm sorry. I didn't realize I was so tired," she says.

"I'm starting to think you wanted this mini vacation a lot more than you let on," I say.

"Maybe."

Her sly smile makes me shake my head.

I round the corner as my Garman instructs, and a large space of perfectly trimmed green grass and tall oak trees stretches out in front of us to our left. Behind it sits a lake. It's so big, I can't tell you where it ends. The truck bounces a bit when the pavement turns to gravel, and a string of cabins appear to our right, the Rocky Mountains displaying the perfect backdrop to the entire picture.

"Oh wow," Abby says when I slow the truck to let three deer leap over the road. It's not uncommon to see deer cross the road in Wyoming, but here, it feels different. More like I'm in their space now.

"Yeah, this is incredible," I say.

I park in a lot outside of the main building and immediately take notice of the many homes that surround the lake. They're spread out enough to give each one plenty of space from their neighbors, but large enough that you can't miss them. The windows alone grab your attention, which no doubt give each one an incredible view, but each house also appears to come fully equipped with a dock as well. These must be these homes Mr. Jinks was talking about and the reason we are here. To sell this atmosphere. I'll tell you, it pretty much sells itself.

Abby meets me around back, climbing into the bed of the truck to hand me our bags.

"There aren't many cars; we must have beat Mr. Jinks here," I say.

Abby stands up straight, and I swear her entire posture goes stiff. "Is he bringing his family?" she asks.

"Just his wife. Why?"

Her shoulders droop and she glances back with a smile. "Just curious if I was going to get a chance to apologize for missing golf."

"Oh, don't worry about that. All is good."

"Let's hurry up and get our room keys so we can check things out by the water before we have to be at dinner," she says

"Sounds good to me."

She slings her backpack over her shoulder and starts to climb down, but the empty strap must catch on something because she slips and I just barely reach her before she falls to the ground. My hands catch her at the hips just perfectly to scrunch up her shirt. My hips are pressed firmly against her own. She might be half falling out of the truck, but I don't miss the way she sucks in a breath as her eyes settle on my lips. I swallow. One move. That's all it would take and I'd be kissing her. One move and everything about this situation would be even more complicated than it is. One move and I'd be a happy man.

Sadly, though, I'm a glutton for punishment, and no matter how much I don't want to stop touching her silky skin or smelling her cinnamon breath, I back up, keeping hold of the backpack for her to slide out of.

"Thanks," she says, her eyes dropping the ground as she grabs her other bag.

"Abby, I …"

"It's fine, Tyler. I totally get it. This is fake, and it needs to stay that way. I can't afford to mess it up either."

She doesn't leave me time to respond before she heads for the main doors.

I let out a long sigh and pack the rest of the bags inside.

I almost tumble over Abby in the entrance. She's frozen in place, taking it all in. I wish I could say I was admiring the lobby too, but all I can focus on is her smile. The one I didn't put there. The one I wish I could ignite every day.

"It's so breathtaking," she says over her shoulder.

"That, it is," I say, but I'm not looking anywhere but at her.

I've never been the kind of person who doesn't know what his next move is, but when I'm with Abby, everything is different. One thing's for sure. These feelings for her aren't going anywhere, and I know she feels them too. At this point, I don't think I'll be able to keep them bottled for much longer.

CHAPTER TEN

Abby

Karma.

That has to be it. I can't imagine any other reason why I'd be in this situation. The last thing Tyler clearly wants is me, so walking into the room we have to share for the weekend and finding only one bed … shoot me now.

Tyler, beside me, is also focused on the bed. The single bed. The one king-size bed that we are supposed to share. Am I obsessing? Yeah, because what the *hell?*

"What's this?" I ask.

"I requested two beds," he says and shrugs. "I can sleep on the couch."

I look away before I roll my eyes. Of course he would. Anything to stay away from Abs.

"Fine."

"Wait." His arm juts out in front of me.

"What?" I push his arm away.

"You're not even going to pretend to offer the bed?" he asks, a small smile touching his lips.

Oh, don't you even ...

"Nope."

He actually has the audacity to look offended. Look here, bucko, you just rejected me in the parking lot. You can sleep on the couch.

Of course, I don't actually say these words to him. It would be pointless. His decision a few minutes ago told me everything I needed to know. I don't stand a chance. Then again ... yep, he's totally thinking of me in my underwear again.

"Tyler?" I snap my fingers.

"Yeah?" He jerks his gaze to mine and actually looks like he has no idea I just caught him checking me out.

"I ..."

Hold up. Tyler is totally attracted to me, yet for some crazy reason, he's pretending that he isn't. Me, on the other hand, I think us is a great idea. Until I get him to see things from my point of view, using this to my advantage might be fun. Drive him a little crazy. Make him see how much he wants me. Sounds like a good time to me.

"Did I sit in something?" I ask. I twist to pop my butt out in front of him and then pretend to look for something myself. My cut-off shorts show plenty of skin but not too much.

"Uh, no." he says and his throat bobs.

"Are you sure?" I ask, running a hand over my right butt cheek to be *sure*.

"I'm sure," he says and backs up. "I'm going to hop in the shower really quick."

A cold shower?

Once he's behind the bathroom door, I let myself smile. This is going to be too easy. Is it mean? Maybe. Him making me think he was going to kiss me and then not was worse.

Running water is the only noise inside the room as I pull clothes from my bag and hang up the ones I don't want wrinkled. I wasn't sure what to pack, so I have a few options for the fancy dinner nights, but in light of this new situation, the two shorter dresses are looking like real winners right now.

I'm just finishing getting a few things out for tonight when there is a knock at the door. I peek though the small circle; Sandy is standing on the other side.

"Hi," I say.

"You guys made it. Great," she says and adjusts the bag on her shoulder. "Since everyone is not here yet, a few of us are meeting up near the sand volleyball net. You two in?"

I look over my shoulder. Tyler's still in the bathroom, but he wouldn't mind.

"Totally in," I say. "Give us ten minutes, and I'll meet you down there?"

"Perfect. Maybe you two can be on my husband's and my team. See you soon."

She turns for the elevator, and before I have the door shut all the way, a hand brushes against my back.

"What are you doing?" Tyler asks, pointing to the open door. His touch hits every part of my body, but my chest seems to enjoy it the most. *Damn.*

I can't stand this close to him.

"Sandy was just here, and I told her we'd … holy naked chest."

Tyler chuckles as I try to figure out where I'm supposed to look. I wasn't expecting him to just walk out of the bathroom topless. I'm the one who's going to play games. Not him. This isn't fair. He's got a solid body, and I just want to touch it. He's so smooth and tan, and I swear his chest is Photoshopped.

Double damn.

"You told her what?" he asks, failing to hide the smile on his lips. His really nice lips. The lips I've always dreamed about kissing, the same exact lips that refused to kiss me.

I shove him back and pass him to the bathroom.

"Put a shirt on. We're playing volleyball in ten minutes. I'll meet you down there." I grab my things off the bed and close myself in the bathroom before he can reply.

He wants to play this game.

I'm in.

Tyler

I'm an ass for not kissing her. I keep avoiding things because I don't want to hurt her, but I do exactly that. I should just man up and tell her exactly how I feel: *Abby, I'm attracted to you. You're hot as fuck and cute as hell all at the same time. I think about you nonstop. I've missed you and because of all that, I don't want to do something that could take all that away from me.*

She'd understand, wouldn't she? She's smart. A whole lot smarter than people give her credit for. I should just tell her.

"Holy shit, Maron. I'm starting to realize why you never told anyone about your fiancée," Rob says from his seat across an unlit fire pit next to the volleyball nets.

I twist in my chair to see exactly what he's talking about.

Holy hell.

Abby is heading our way with a giant grin. She's wearing a pair of high-waisted shorts that make her legs look extra long with a soft green crop top under a blue and white jacket thing, that I honestly don't know what its purpose is as it slips off her shoulders. Her hair is pulled back into a side braid, and she looks fucking stunning.

I can't take my eyes of off her. Off her smile. Off the way her attention is solely on me.

By the time I pick my jaw up off the sand, I notice that I'm not the only guy staring at her. Fuck. If this is the response she gets by just wearing this outfit, I don't even want to know how they react when they see her in a bikini.

Actually, I won't know, because I'm pretty sure right now, right this moment, any water activities are off the schedule for me and Abby.

"Hey," she says, grinning up at me when I meet her halfway. "What's with the look?" she points to my face and then looks behind her.

"Nothing," I say, and I hope to God I manage to put some other expression on my face. Anything that isn't hinting how caveman I'm about to go.

I clear my throat. "Why'd you change?"

"Because it's hot out and I want to be comfortable."

"Well … you forgot the other half of your shorts" is the most genius thing I can come up with.

Abby laughs and then leans into me. Cucumber is all I can smell.

"Does my outfit bother you?'

"No," I answer quickly. Probably too quickly. I look past her to find something else to focus on. Yes. Good. The kid wiping down the paddleboard. Great.

Abby lifts to her tiptoes, and her breath brushes across my neck as she whispers, "I think it does."

I shake my head.

Her laughter goes straight to my groin.

"I wonder what else I can do to get you all worked up," she says right before she heads toward the others with small skips. She grins over her shoulder, and thank God she's far enough away that she doesn't hear me growl.

I'm trying to maintain some self-control, but she's making it hard. Both mentally and physically.

"Tyler, are you in on this game?" Sandy asks.

"Eh, I might sit this one out," I say. I need to pull myself together.

"Of course he will," Abby says. "He hates losing." Her flirtatious tone releases a small chuckle.

"I wouldn't lose," I say.

She fails at not smiling as she shrugs. "I guess we'll never know."

"I wouldn't."

"If you say so."

"Abby," I warn.

"Tyler," she says softly, and that does it.

"I'm in." I hop out of my seat. "You're going down."

"We'll see," she says.

"Okay, Sandy and Abby versus Tyler and Rob," Sandy's husband calls out.

"Yes!" Abby cheers and high-fives Sandy. "They are toast."

"Enjoy your happiness now; it won't last long," I say.

"Ha ha, funny," Abby replies picking up the ball. "Ladies first."

She tosses the ball back to Sandy, who is ready to serve.

"We've got this," I say to Rob. He just shakes his head.

"If you say so, but I've never been real big on this game."

Sandy tosses the ball up and smacks it with the palm of her hand. It flies straight for Rob, who bends to hit it. He hits it so hard, it not only makes it back over the net but out of bounds.

"Shoot," he says. "Sorry, Tyler. It's been a while."

"It's fine," I say and shake it off.

Sandy and Abby celebrate their first point and get into position. The ball speeds over the next, this time right for me. I bump it perfectly to return it. Sandy taps it and Abby leaps up, spiking it back to my side. Sand sprays into my face as the ball lands in front of me.

I hear the girls cheering again.

What the heck is Rob doing?

Then I see it. He's watching Abby and grinning like a boy in high school with a crush.

No.

No.

This is not happening.

"Rob!" He jumps.

"What's up?"

"What're you doing?" I ask.

He shrugs. "I'm not good at this sport."

"Clearly."

"It's just a game. Besides, look how excited they are to be winning by a whole two points."

Abby is doing a little dance. Her hips sway and she laughs at something Sandy says.

I swear my heart tightens. She looks so carefree.

She turns my direction, so I pull my attention away.

Everyone takes their spot, but this time, I'm not so ready. I'm thinking Rob might be on to something.

The ball sails over the net and when I miss, I'm not upset that I'm about to lose.

Abby erupts into a fit of laughter.

That's when I lose all self-control.

"Holy crap, Ty—" she starts, cutting herself off as I duck under the net and head her way. She backs up, looking around briefly before her gaze connects with mine.

She knows what's about to happen. I know she knows and yet, the small gasp she makes right before my lips press against hers ignites my core. I kiss her hard, wrapping my arms around her waist to lift her and keep her body as close to mine as possible. Her arms circle around my neck to hold me as tightly as she can as she lets out a small groan.

I love it. I love everything about the way she feels in my arms, against my body, and the way her skin feels as I stroke her back.

I start to lower her feet back to the ground, but stop when she squeezes me tighter, her tongue forcing its way through my lips to tangle with my own. My eyes are closed, but I swear I see sparks. They zing throughout my entire body, reaching every inch, waking me to feel something I've never felt before. A kiss I've never experienced before.

Slowly, she gains her balance, pulling back to look up at me.

Her eyes are brighter now as she catches her breath.

"Holy shit," she says, her fingers touching her lips as she watches me.

Holy shit is right.

I just kissed my best friend.

I want to do it again.

But … I can't lose her again.

And yet I just gave her more ammunition to avoid me. Women who are trying to turn their life around do not appreciate guys who want to lead them right back to the original sin.

CHAPTER ELEVEN

Abby

Ohmygod. Ohmygod. Ohmygod.

Tyler kissed me.

He full on lip locked and tongue tangoed with me right in front of his coworkers.

Holy crap!

I take a deep breath and sit on the couch in our bedroom. Tyler went to confirm our dinner reservations with the restaurant. He said he wanted to make sure the time hasn't changed.

I'm actually glad he had to go, because I need a moment to process this. Was it all for appearance's sake? I mean, it didn't feel that way. Was it just an apology kiss for earlier today? No, it couldn't have been. Then again, if that's his apology, he can mess up more often. Or was it … real?

God, and the way his hands tickled my back. Goose bumps, the good kind, touch every inch of my skin. I want him to do that again so much. I wouldn't mind if he did more than just kiss me.

Christ, Abby. It was just one kiss. One kiss doesn't mean anything.

I'm overthinking.

I just need to take a deep breath and let it out slowly.

There, that's better.

Tonight's dinner is supposed to be fancy. I brought a black dress for it. It's a loaner dress from Beth. It's tight. Form fitting, as Beth called it. The left shoulder is cut out and the right side has a slit that goes about mid-thigh. It's sexy, I think. Yes, I brought it for a reason and after that volleyball game, I'm thinking the dress is going to work out a lot better than originally planned.

The sun moves lower in the sky, creating a perfect shine over the lake beyond my window. The sun and the lake are all this place needs to look as beautiful as it does. Or maybe I'm just seeing things differently now.

Me and Tyler. I've wanted this for so long that now that it's here … I mean, did he actually kiss me? Or have I wanted this for so long that I finally fell off the crazy boat and imagined the entire thing?

I shake my head. I didn't imagine it. It happened.

If dinner is still at seven, I have only a couple hours to get ready. After playing in the sand and getting it in places it doesn't need to be, a shower is definitely the way to go. I grab my towel that I'd hung off the closet door and head for the bathroom.

I twist the shower knob to hot, letting the steam fog the mirrors and warm up the room. I've learned that shaving is almost pointless if I'm just going to step out of the shower into a cold room. Tonight, I don't want shaving my legs to be pointless.

The water cascades over my skin, and my shoulders instantly drop. If Tyler were in here with me, would he want the water hot or cold?

I shove my face under the water.

Cool it, Abby. For fuck's sake. All he did was kiss you.

I shave my legs in record time and turn the shower off. I need to stay busy so my mind won't wander.

Hanging the towel on its designated hook, I prop one foot against the tub and grab my lotion.

The last thing I'm expecting when I bend forward to start at my ankle is for the bathroom door to hit me in the butt. It smacks my bare ass and sends me diving into the tub.

"What the—?" I shout as I go down. Not ladylike, but hell, all chances of ladylike was gone the moment my rear went into the air.

"Shit, shit, shit," Tyler says behind me.

"Tyler!" I shout and twist as quickly as I can into the fetal position. My hands flail, trying to decide what is more important to cover because holy hell, I'm naked. This is not a flattering angle in any way.

I'm expecting Tyler to either cover his eyes or turn away, but instead, I find him staring and smiling. His smile is so freaking cute, too, I can't even be that mad.

He starts to laugh, which only causes me to do the same.

"At least get me a towel if you're going to just stand there," I say, and he nods.

He tosses one my way and faces the opposite direction.

"I'm sorry. I should have looked away sooner, but I just couldn't. Abby, do you even know how fucking sexy you are? I mean … and then with your ass …" He clears his throat.

I crawl out of the tub, wrap myself up, and try not

the let the enormous smile on my face stretch my cheeks. But when I look to Tyler, waiting for him to finish his sentence, I don't miss the way his posture stiffens.

"Dinner is still at the same time," he says and walks out of the bathroom.

What just happened?

* * *

Tyler hasn't said much since we left to go to dinner.

I thought I was going to get a little something—a hug, a peck on the cheek even—when I walked out of the bathroom after putting on my dress, but all I got was a little wide-eyed look, a bottom lip drop, and then a groan. I wanted him to kiss me again, but seeing him struggle to keep his eyes a normal size was nice too.

We take the elevator down and Tyler touches my lower back. What girl doesn't enjoy that? Lacing our hands isn't so bad either. Confusing as hell, but not bad.

"Perfect timing," Sandy says as we step into the restaurant. She and her husband are waiting at the podium to be seated. "You look absolutely stunning," she says as she surveys my dress.

"Yes, she does," Tyler says, beating me to a response. But he isn't looking my way. He's focusing on the tables just inside.

"Thank you," I say to Sandy and brush up against Tyler. I wrap my arms around his waist and kiss his cheek.

He lets out a deep breath and drops his chin.

"Abby, we need to talk."

"Your table is ready," the hostess says before Tyler can say more.

I don't release our embrace until we begin to take our seats.

Sandy and her husband are mid sit when they see someone they know and excuse themselves, leaving Tyler and I alone at the table until someone else arrives.

"Look, Abby." He doesn't waste any time. My heart feels like a walnut on the floor that someone stepped on. I have a good hunch I don't want to hear what he has to say.

"I'm sorry about earlier today."

"Which part?"

"Abs," he says in a soft tone, reaching for my hand. "We both knew what we're getting into when we agreed to this. We can't let anything cloud our judgment to keep this simple."

"You mean we can't let our feelings get involved?"

If he isn't going to be specific, I will.

He nods.

"It's a little late for that, isn't it? I mean when you kissed me, it—"

"Was just for show and didn't mean anything," he says quickly.

I don't need a mirror to know my mouth is hanging open as I stare at him. I knew this could be a possibility, but I didn't want it to be the truth.

"Sorry about that," Sandy says, taking her seat across from me. "Did you two decide on an appetizer?"

I blink, gaze down to the table, and inhale. For so many years I've wanted to be someone he *wanted*.

Reality is a bitch.

Dinner on our first night has only just begun. There is no

way I can hold back the tears fighting their way out for two more days.

Yet, somehow, right now, I keep them at bay and plaster a smile on my face. After all, it's all just for show.

Tyler

"Did you see Allison's dress? Holy shit," Abby whispers, pulling her leg through my bedroom window. "I mean, I hate to say it, but she definitely wanted attention."

"Ah, yeah, were you not there when she faked trying to fix the strap of her shoe? She physically paused and bent over to look back at Logan," I say, gripping the back of my shirt and yanking it over my head. "She was there with a purpose tonight."

"She failed," Abby says, deadpan.

I twist to see what's changed her tone; she's zoning out.

"Abs." I snap my fingers.

"Yeah," she says, her gaze flashing up to mine.

"Are you okay? Did you drink too much? Shit, you aren't going to throw up like you did after Derrick's last party, are you?" I ask.

She shakes her head. "No, I didn't really drink tonight. Going home buzzed isn't my best move right now."

"Is your mom still seeing that one guy?" I ask. What I really want to ask is why is your mom still being a snatch, *but for obvious reasons, I don't.*

Abby answers with a small nod, grabbing the shorts and shirt I toss on the bed for her and stepping into my bathroom.

Abby's mom behaves the way Abby should. Like a seventeen-year-old girl who just wants to have fun. It makes life hard for Abby, but that's why she has me. Best friends take care of each other, right?

Besides, it's not like people don't know about her mom. Not to say her mom is the talk of the town, but my parents know enough that they let Abby sleep over sometimes. The last few months it's been more nights than usual. I don't think her mom even knows she doesn't come home.

I switch out my jeans to my Nike basketball shorts before I knock on the bathroom door.

"Abs, you okay in there?" I ask. It's dumb. I know. But I feel helpless for her.

"I'm fine," she says, swinging the door open.

I wrap my arms around her and hold tightly. "You can always count on me. Don't forget that."

"I won't," she says, pulling out of my grip.

My hands are still locked around her, holding her in place, when she pauses, our mouths just inches apart. I take a breath and she closes her eyes.

A tap at my window jolts us away from each other. I dash over to lift the frame and pull Kelsey inside.

"I'll admit, sneaking over here when there isn't any snow on the ground is a lot easier," she says, kicking off her shoes. "What's going on?" she asks.

I glance to Abby, who is now crawling into my bed, and then back to Kelsey. I mouth the word mom, *and she nods. Then, since she came over already in her pajamas, my girlfriend crawls into my bed with my best friend.*

I make my makeshift bed on the floor next to them and look up. Abby is watching me. The blank expression on her face makes my heart pound.

Kissing Abby ... not my worst idea.

Kissing Abby while I'm still dating Kelsey and ruining our friendship ... that's an idea I never want to imagine.

I think I finally know what Abby's signature blank expression means.

Tyler sucks.

She's right, too.

I'm a horrible person.

I'm a royal jackass.

Abby hasn't spoken the entire ride up to the room, and I don't blame her.

I'm sure she's just as eager to get inside the room so we don't have to pretend anymore. Maybe then she'll let me know exactly what she's thinking or feeling. We can talk this out, but no matter what, I have to do my best not to cave and take back what I said. I have to stick with it if we want this to work out. And if I don't want to lose my best friend.

I slide the key into the slot and lift. Red lights. I do the same thing. More red lights. It happens again on the third.

"Jesus, Tyler," Abby says, jerking the room card from my hand and shoving it into the door. When she pulls it back, the green light appears, and the door opens.

She storms in, tossing her clutch on the couch and then closing the door behind her once she's in the bathroom.

I stand frozen in the entryway.

I'm in unfamiliar territory here. One the one hand, I want to stay and talk to her—on the other hand, it might be easier if I just leave and gave her some space.

Closing the door, I decide to wait on the couch.

I sit.

I wait.

There's no noise coming from the bathroom.

I keep sitting.

The shower starts.

I take this as my cue to leave.

Retreating down the elevator, I hang my head low.

What am I doing? I should be up there waiting for her and telling her how sorry I am and that I didn't mean anything I said. That kiss wasn't for show. Unless you count showing everyone she's mine and off limits.

The doors open to the lobby, and I'm tempted to close them, ride back up, and force her to talk to me. I don't want us to go back to never speaking or only speaking to each other harshly. I hated that, and remembering the kind of friendship we used to have, well, I messed that up more times then I want to remember.

This time, I'm going to fix it before it gets worse.

CHAPTER TWELVE

Abby

I slept like shit. No thanks to Tyler. Then again, I'm at fault too. I keep thinking something between Tyler and I could still happen. I'm legit crazy. How is it even possible for my brain to still think this is possible? He's had more than a decade to develop feelings for me—what makes me think he could suddenly realize them now?

For one, the fact that I don't believe the kiss was just for show. Two, he held my hand tightly last night, as if his grip were to loosen, I would float away. It definitely wasn't like the limp fish grip he had at the picnic a couple weeks ago.

The part that sealed it? Tyler came back to the room and he could have just climbed into bed, pulled up the covers, and fallen asleep, but no. He snuggled up and held me.

Pulled me close.

Kissed the back of my shoulder.

I should have pushed him away, but I didn't want to.

"Where's Tyler?" Rob asks as he focuses on the waves

brushing against the boat. Today the company has planned to take us around the lake, stopping for lunch at a picnic area on the other side. The sun is hot, there isn't a breeze, and the people, aside from the one I came with, are great.

"I think he went below to get something to drink," I answer.

"Ah," Rob says, leaning over the railing the way I am and gazing down at the water. "You two okay?"

"Is it that obvious?" I ask.

"Yes and no. The tension is noticeable, but at this point it's hard to tell if it's from anger or attraction. The lack of a smile on your face though gives the real answer away."

I force a smile.

"Yeah, no, that's not real."

His comment makes me grin in fact this time.

"There we go," he says. "You should do that more often. You have a beautiful smile."

"Thank you."

Rob is a nice guy. Too nice sometimes. He's the exact opposite of the type of men I usually go for. He seems genuinely interested in how I'm doing right now. I never pick guys who care like that. I pick selfish and rude. The same kind of men my mother picks.

"Do you want to talk about it?" Rob asks, and for a moment I debate actually sharing something—not the truth, but something. However, Tyler catches my eye. He's watching my interaction with Rob. He's standing stiff and his arms are crossed.

Good.

Be mad.

Jealous.

Whatever.

I don't care.

Rob twists to look behind him.

"I'll give you two a moment, but if you ever need someone to talk to, come find me."

He pats my shoulders as he heads in the opposite direction of Tyler.

I see Tyler approaching out of the corner of my eye but keep my focus on the small waves the boat creates.

"What did he want?" Tyler asks.

"We were just talking."

"Talking or flirting?"

"Are you being serious?" I snap. "You do not get to treat me the way you have the last two days and then be jealous when another man talks to me. You said it was all for show. That's it. Oh wait, is this for show too? Acting jealous?"

"Abby," he starts, but I hold up my hand.

"Not right now, Tyler. I don't want to do this in front of people."

His jawline flexes as he clenches his teeth. "Fine. We're pulling up for the lunch. Let's go talk."

It's a lose-lose situation. We get off this boat and fight and make it worse and then have to ride back still mad, or I don't go talk to him and we ride the boat back still mad. Unless I just go along with everything he says and pretend I'm not affected by him.

Tyler grabs my hand. Everyone else is assisting unload coolers, but he just marches us right on by them all.

"Tyler, we should stop to help."

"Nope."

"Don't you think that's rude?"

"I have other things to be more worried about."

"Sure you do."

His only response is to keep walking until we can no longer hear the faint chatter of the group.

The little island we're on is a mix of beach and trees and giant boulders. Tyler finds a boulder big enough to shield us, and stops.

"How can I fix this?"

I shrug. "You'll figure it out."

"Come on, Abby, just be honest for once and tell me what you want."

"I'm not being honest? Just me? You're the one who can't admit his own feelings!" I shout and turn to head back.

"Don't walk away from me," he says, grabbing my wrist and spinning me to face me.

"Why not? It's not like you're going to doing or say anything to make this better."

"You don't think I want to? You don't think that every goddamn moment of this entire trip I haven't thought about kissing you? Kissing you more than I did on the sand yesterday. About touching you. About being alone with you and showing you exactly how I feel. News flash, Abs—that's all I can freaking think about!" He makes an exploding gesture from his temples. "I'm going out of my mind by not doing a single thing."

I cross my hands to cover the way my chest is heaving to breathe, especially now that I, too, can only think about him touching me. Or me ... kissing him. Slapping him. Holding him.

Meanwhile, he paces and pulls at his hair. He has no idea

what to do. But I could take away his stress and control the situation.

"Do it. Do all those things and more." I take a step closer to him. "*Kiss* me." Another step. "*Touch* me." Standing as close as I can without contact, I whisper, "We're alone now, Tyler. Show me."

He captures my lips with his own, his hands on each side of my face as the pressure of his kiss increases. He backs me up to the rock, pushing into me. His hands move from my cheeks to my shoulders and down, until he's able to grip my waist, lifting me to wrap my legs around him.

"God, this feels good," he moans as his lips kiss down to my neck. "Is this what you wanted?"

"Yes," I breathe.

"You want me to kiss you here?" He kisses my collarbone.

"Yes."

He kisses between my breasts. "Here?"

"Yes."

"What else do you want?" he asks.

"More. Just more."

His lips return to mine more eagerly than before.

My hands bunch his shirt as I hold on to him, squeezing my legs to pull him closer.

"Damn it, Abby," he groans. "This is exactly why I didn't do this. I don't know if I can stop."

A bubble of laughter erupts out of my chest.

"What?" he asks.

"We aren't fooling around against a rock," I tell him straight up. "I mean, any more than we already have."

A smile slowly appears on his lips as he surveys the space

around us. Then, he chuckles too, loosening his grip to let my feet drop to the ground.

"Good idea."

I straighten out my clothes and run my hand through my hair.

"Should we head back?" I ask. "Or should we actually talk instead of just kissing?"

Tyler instantly plops on to the sand and pats the seat next to him.

"Let's talk," he says.

Crossing one leg over the other, I sit back on my hands to soak in the sun.

"We could start with you telling me about the rehab mail I saw on your table the other day," Tyler says.

My entire body goes stiff.

Shit.

"I …" I stop. Of all the things he could ask me right now, that's what he chooses? "It's none of your business."

"I know, but, Abby, if you have a problem, I want to—"

"I don't have a problem and we aren't talking about this," I say.

"Abby, if you—"

"Stop."

"I just—"

"Stop!" I shout, and, thankfully, this time he doesn't respond. He doesn't even say anything when I get up and walk away.

Good.

No matter how many late nights we had in high school and no matter how many times he told me my life would be better when I could legally move away from her, I don't want him to know I'm still in the same exact spot as when we were teenagers.

It used to be so easy sharing my life with Tyler, and now it's complicated. If we were truly meant to be more, wouldn't it still be easy?

"Everything okay?" Sandy asks as I arrive where the food is set up.

"I'm fine."

It's true.

It has to be.

As of this moment, I have to be just fine, and I have to accept that the idea of Tyler and I is just that. An idea.

Tyler

When things in my life are unsteady, I usually turn to work as a distraction, but tonight, it's failing.

I glance over my computer screen to the bathroom door and tap my pen on the table.

Abby's been in there for almost an hour.

It doesn't take a genius to know that she's avoiding me. Unless she needed to for the sake of appearances, she's done her best to avoid speaking with me since we returned from lunch. Now we're preparing for dinner with Sandy and her husband.

Or, at least, I've been ready for the last hour.

I was hoping we'd have time to chat some things out or have enough time for me to apologize and tell her … I don't know … that I'm going to say and do stupid stuff from time to time but that I want her to stick around even when I do.

That sounds so lame.

I groan, scrubbing my hands over my face. What the hell am I going to say? I don't want this to be how it is. I want more.

The door opens, and I close my laptop and stand, all in one motion.

"Hey." I close my mouth instantly

Holy shit.

"You look … stunning."

She forces a grin. "Thanks, Tyler. Should we go?"

"Yeah," I say. She practically glides across the room in her blue strappy heels and nude dress. I have no idea what kind of dress it is, but the way it hugs her chest and waist before fluffing out at her hips … she should wear this dress every damn day.

"Are you coming?" she asks, holding the door open.

Do it. Just say whatever comes out. You can't let her walk out that door without trying.

"Yes, but before we go, I want to talk to you."

"Tyler, please, just—"

"I don't want to be only a friend to you, Abby. I want more."

She lets the door close, crosses her arms, and leans back against the wall.

"I overstepped today, but I care about you. So much. And I know you said you're swearing off men, but I never expected to have the feelings I have for you, and I can't just ignore them. I don't want to. And I know you're mad at me, but—"

"I'm not mad at you," she says.

"You're not?"

"No. I mean, mad isn't the right word," she says.

"Then what is?"

"Frustrated … maybe. Annoyed. Confused."

"Hard to pick just one, huh?"

"When it comes to you, yes."

This isn't working out how I wanted.

"Being straight forward about what I want is a good approach, don't you think?" I ask, stepping toward her.

"I guess so."

"Fine. I want to be with you as more than friends. Not just today or while we're here this weekend, but for as long as you let me."

"Are you serious?" she asks, her mouth twisting to the side as she holds back a smile.

"Completely." I swoop her into my arms and pressing my mouth against hers.

Call me an animal. Call me sadistic. I don't care. I want her so completely distracted, she can't even think clearly enough to speak, let alone think about speaking. I want her to lose control and I want to be the one to do that to her.

I press my mouth to hers, hard. I meet my tongue to hers and she moans. I repeat the motion, this time pressing my hips into her. She moans louder.

Yes. This is what I want.

I break away from her, her hands lingering between us, beckoning me to return to her—and I will, just not yet.

"We're going to be late for dinner," I tell her.

"I'm not hungry anymore," she says, pressing a soft kiss to my lips.

Damn.

"Keep that up and we won't make it."

"I …" is all she gets out before there is knock at the door.

Sandy and her husband are in the room next to us, so it's no surprise when I open the door to find them waiting for us.

"You two ready?" Sandy asks.

"One sec. Let me double-check my lipstick," Abby says, blushing as her gaze flashes to mine briefly.

"So, did you hear?" Sandy asks while we wait.

"Hear what?"

"That Mr. Jinks's kid showed up and made a huge scene about not having a room ready while we were out on the boat."

Great. Fucking Kurt. That's the last thing I need.

"Okay, I'm ready," Abby says, beaming all her teeth as she heads toward us.

How does she know Kurt? Or maybe she doesn't and Kurt was just trying to get under my skin. No. He had to have been talking about Abby.

"Are you good?" Abby asks when I don't move.

"Yeah," I say and follow her out the door.

Until I find the right moment to ask Abby how she knows him or if she does, steering clear of him is definitely the way to go.

"How do you guys feel about dinner away from the resort tonight?" I ask inside the elevator.

"Sounds fine to me," Sandy says, and her husband nods.

I lace my hand with Abby's. "Does that work for you?"

"Yep." She nods.

I don't care that we have an audience. I lean down and kiss her.

No one is ruining my night.

CHAPTER THIRTEEN

Abby

I typically enjoy rain, but on days like today, when I'd planned to spend the day lying next to the water and soaking up the sun, I loathe it.

"What indoor activities do they have?" I ask.

Tyler snorts.

"I set myself up for that one."

"Yes, you did," he says, stepping out of the bathroom and kissing me on the forehead.

When I first woke up this morning, I'll admit I thought *this is when Tyler freaks out and goes all "I can't do this" on me*, but so far, that isn't on his agenda for today.

"Do you want to order in some breakfast? Or do you want to go down to the restaurant?" he asks.

"How about I run downstairs and bring us back something?" I offer.

"Perfect. I want French toast," he says.

"Perfect," I mimic his tone and grab my room key before heading out the door.

The elevators open to the lobby and as I step out, my heart plummets into my stomach. I try to casually turn and step back in before he sees me.

"Abby."

Shit. Shit. I failed.

"You are just the person I was looking for."

Every hair on my body rises. If Kurt is looking for someone, it's not good.

I thought he wasn't supposed to be here this weekend.

Slowly, I turn back around and fake a smile. "What can I do for you?"

Oh god, I hope my voice didn't shake the way I am on the inside.

"Should we grab a drink?" he asks and points to the restaurant.

"It's eleven in the morning," I say.

"A soda then?" The grin he'd been sporting goes flat as he leans in. "You're going to sit with me whether you like it or not."

"Abby, hey," Sandy says, passing us as she, too, heads for the restaurant.

I smile and wave.

"You wouldn't want to draw attention, would you?" Kurt mumbles just loudly enough for me to hear.

"I'll give you five minutes."

"That's all I need."

I follow Kurt and the hostess to a table and find a seat that lets me keep an eye on anyone who approaches us. It also gives me a good view of the restaurant's exit. Just in case I need to dash out of here. Which I'd love to do more than anything right now.

"How's your mother?" he asks.

"She's fine. No thanks to you."

"It's not my fault she sampled the product she was supposed to be delivering and got caught."

"She shouldn't have been delivering anything."

"And you think that's my fault."

"Yes."

"Hmm, well, let's agree to disagree and get to the point of my visit. You mother did a job for me and now that she is unreachable, I need someone to fill her place."

"This is stupid. I'm leaving." I stand.

The silverware and glasses rattle as his fist connects with table before he scoots his chair back. "You will sit, and you will listen."

The room has gone silent. People are staring.

I sit.

Without being obvious, I survey the room. Where is Sandy? Did she see that? Someone will know something isn't right if she saw that. Except she's nowhere to be found.

"I want you to take your mom's place. I have everything you'll need in my car, and I need you to get started tonight."

I laugh. "No."

"You will not tell me no."

"I will tell you no. I'm not doing this. Find someone else."

"You're the reason I'm in this situation."

"No, you're the reason you're in this situation."

This time when I stand, I'm prepared for an outburst, but instead, he rises and a smug grin stitches across his face.

"If you don't do this, I can promise you, you will hate yourself by the time I'm done with you."

"Well, I guess I'll just have to live with that," I say and return to the elevator.

The only thing Kurt and I have in common that he could use against me is my mother and—news flash! I'm not her favorite person. Anything he thinks he can do won't even faze me.

Tyler

"Let's go home," Abby says, pressing the hotel door closed behind her. I'm in the middle of an email to a client, but I close my laptop. "The fireworks have always been so amazing on the lake in Wind Valley, and you know it's sort of like tradition, and I think I've seen them from the exact spot for the last five years, maybe more, and I just don't think I should—"

"Whoa, whoa, slow down," I say, pulling her into my arms. "Is everything okay?" I ask.

"Fine. Great. Dandy. Why?"

I step back and look her up and down.

Why's she being so weird?

"Something's up," I say.

"No."

"Then where is the food?"

"Oh, um ..." She glances back at the door and then at her hands. Her head snaps up. "The line downstairs was crazy long, so I thought we'd just order from up here after all."

I don't believe her.

"Abby, what's going on? And why do you want to go home?"

"I just don't want to skip out on a memory I've had for so long." She shrugs and sits on the bed, watching me.

I hold her hand in mine as I sit next to her.

"Old memories are good, I agree," I say and kiss her knuckles. "But new ones … I can't wait to make those with you."

I capture her lips with mine and wrap my arms around her waist.

"If going home is really what you want, we can do that. I don't care either way as long as I'm with you."

"Really?"

"Yes."

Her gaze drifts from mine for moment, then she nods.

"Okay. We can stay."

I kiss her once more before she pushes me away.

"Let's order some food. I'm hungry."

* * *

"I love fireworks," I say and clap my hands together.

"Yeah," Abby mumbles next to me as we walk toward the resort's events cabin. Earlier, she'd said she was fine staying, and she was even her normal self while we hung out in the room, but ever since we left, it's like she's distracted. Or maybe looking for someone, since she keeps glancing behind us.

"Something on your mind?" I ask.

"No."

Sure there isn't.

"Are you sure? Because you know I'm here for you."

After a long sigh she says, "You remember my mom, right?"

"How could I not?"

Abby's mouth wrinkles to the side.

"Sorry."

"No, you're right. When you're the world's shittiest mom, people don't forget."

"Anyway," I say and place my hand on her back. "What's going on?"

"She's just, still the same old mom, and it's exhausting."

"Yeah, but you're an adult now." I kiss the top of her head. "You don't have to go home to her every night."

"No, but she's still my mom."

True. Just like in high school, I'll never know what Abby's mom's deal is. How could she not like Abby?

"I just wish she'd finally figure things out and actually be a mother," Abby says, and the sadness in her voice stops me.

"Hey." I twist her to face me. "Do you want to hang around other people right now?"

"I mean, I'm not feeling particularly social, no, but I'll do it for you. That's why I'm here."

"That's how I got you here, yeah. But that's not why you're here," I say and curl her under my arm. "Let's ditch this place and watch the fireworks from our room. We can order up some drinks, maybe some cheesecake, and sit out on the balcony."

"Yeah?" she asks, and her eyes light up.

"Yeah."

We turn back for the resort and my chest swells at the

smile on Abby's face. That's the expression I want to see every day.

"Where are you two headed?" Sandy asks, pausing with a blanket folded in her arms.

"Back to the room," I say without stopping.

Abby laughs and slaps my chest. "You could have stopped to talk."

"Nope."

"Mmm hmm."

"Yeah, yeah, let's just get back to the room before the show starts."

* * *

The cheesecake is ordered, the drinks are in hand—thanks to Abby's genius idea to grab them on the way up to the room—and it's just the two of us sitting on our balcony under the stars, waiting for the fireworks to start.

And Abby … god, she's only wearing a pair of shorts with one of my hoodies, but she looks incredible. I'll never forget the first night she stayed at my house. I'd lent her a T-shirt and shorts, and when she walked out of the bathroom, this sense of pride, maybe, or newfound confidence came over me. I liked that she was wearing my clothes. That she was in my house. My room. That I was the person she'd come to when she needed someone. I'd also vowed in that moment that I'd never let her down.

Somehow, over the years, I did though.

"Hey," I say and reach for her chair. With one tug, I drag her seat closer to mine.

"Ooh, I wasn't close enough before?'

"Definitely not." I tilt her chin up and press my lips against hers.

The first set of fireworks scream into the air. We pull away from each other just in time to see red, blue, and green sparks exploding above the small island they're being shot from.

Abby flinches when a thunderous purple burst against the night sky. I pull her tight and kiss the side of her head.

Another string of booms sounds, but I can't tell you where they ended up in the sky.

Abby's placed her hand on my thigh and I can't pull my eyes away from the way she tickles the top of my leg.

Is she staring at her hand like I am?

I chance a glance.

Nope.

She's watching the fireworks.

If she can focus, I can focus. This is simple.

Holy shit.

She's moving her hand up.

How is she still watching the show and not distracted by this?

"Are you going to keep sitting there staring at me, or are you going to make a move? Because I've got to tell you, fireworks and—"

I don't know what she was going to say and I'm never going to know. I capture her lips with my own, my hands cupping her face to deepen the kiss and pull her to me. She leans as far as she can before my grip drops to her hips, tugging her to the edge of her chair and guiding her in front of me. Never breaking our mouths, she straddles my knees and sinks into my lap.

I squeeze her butt to inch her closer, allowing her the connection she needs to grind her hips into mine.

"Fuck yes," I say and kiss her cheek, her neck, moving lower with each touch of my lips. If I had known that kissing Abby and touching her like this was going to make my body feel like it was buzzing with electricity, I'd have done this back in junior high when I first wanted to and I'd have been on cloud nine for my entire life.

The gasp she makes as her body bends, her breasts pushing into my face, sets me on fire, awakening every part of me. I know the moment she feels it.

"Oh my god," she says, grabbing my face and kissing me hard.

Locking my hands under her thighs, I move us from the balcony to the bedroom.

Slowly, I lower her onto the bed, spreading her knees and kneeling between them. I kiss her stomach, her hips, and then I unbutton her shorts, all while inching her sweater higher with my other hand.

She lifts herself off the bed as I slide her shorts down her legs.

"Jesus, Tyler. I don't think I want you to take this slow. I don't care if I sound slutty. Get me naked."

"As much as I want that too, I don't want to rush this."

"Fuck," she moans. Sitting up quickly, she scoots the end of the bed. Her hands are on my belt before I can even consider slowing her down.

"Fast this time and the next we can take slow," she says gazing up as me as her hands make quick work with my pants.

She's got a point.

On her cue, we both quickly strip the remainder of our clothes.

I crawl over her, forcing her to inch back toward the pillows. Her gaze locks on mine the entire time. When she stops, I slide my hand down the side of her leg, gripping her thigh and pulling it open to make room for myself.

Fuck. Her skin is like velvet. I could run my hands along every piece of her all day long.

"Damn, Abby," I say, but that's all I get out before she pulls me down to kiss her. Slowly, our tongues stroke together. I settle further between her legs, feeling the breath she releases across my lips when we touch.

Her hand skirts from my shoulder down to my waist, moving between us to grip me.

I suck in a breath.

Shit, that feels fucking unreal.

I kiss her harder as she strokes me. I definitely won't last long at the rate we're going. I have to stop her.

I slowly remove her hand and return the favor. I slide one finger in, then two, and her head falls back into the pillows.

"Tyler."

Fuck me. I was never that great at foreplay.

I retract my fingers and place myself at her core before she can say a word.

Steadily, pacing myself, I slide into her.

"God, Tyler, you feel so good," she moans, her back bowing into me.

Fueled by the noises she makes, I grind my hips slower and deeper. My body feels like it's electrified with each thrust. Being this connected with Abby ... I've never felt it with anyone else before. It's out of this world.

The way her body squeezes me makes mine move faster.

"Yes, keep doing that. Harder," she instructs.

Before I know it, she's crying out my name as I cry out hers.

I drop to her side, kissing her temple as we catch our breath.

I just had sex with my best friend. It's either the best thing I've ever done, or the stupidest.

Right now, I don't care about the what-ifs.

Right now, I have everything I need. Nothing can take this away from me.

CHAPTER FOURTEEN

Abby

Sex with Tyler is incredible. The only thing that could be better would be if I could eat anything I ever wanted and never gain weight.

Last night was like I was living in a different world. And I've never woken up in someone's arms and wanted to stay there.

I wasn't a virgin last night, but the few times I have fooled around with someone and slept in their bed, well, I was too uneasy to sleep. Therefore, I'd never let them get close enough to cuddle. Tyler is different. I fell asleep right away with him, and having him hold me makes me feel safe.

Oh my god, I sound so lame.

Don't be lame, Abby.

"Good morning," Tyler whispers, and his warm breath skirts over my shoulder, sending a wave of pebbles over my skin. He presses a soft kiss against my neck, and if I wasn't completely awake before, I sure as hell am now.

"Morning," I say back and twist under his hold to face him.

Tyler smiles wide as his gaze racks over my face.

"God, I never in a million years thought I'd be waking up to this face," he says.

"That bad, huh?" I ask, holding back my smile.

"Horrible," he says. "Worst thing I've ever seen."

I push away from him as his deep laughter surrounds me. He tugs me back until my body is flush against his.

"Your face," he kisses my forehead, "is the most perfect way to wake up."

"Is it now?" My hand touches his bare hip, and I can feel the goose bumps the moment they appear, but I don't stop. I follow the ridges of his six pack and lower my touch until I hear his sharp inhale.

"Is it better than this?" I ask.

"Mmm hmm," he says. His eyes press closed, and his hips twitch closer to me. "Fuck," he groans when I've taken him in my hand.

With slow strokes, he begins to fall apart.

At the next groan, I move my hand faster. His entire body jerks up as he pushes my hand away, circles his arms around me, and flips me onto my back.

"If you keep that up, I'll be done before we even get started."

Tyler goes straight for my chest, kissing each nipple, hardening them until I'm pulling at my hair and saying his name on repeat.

"I love hearing you say my name," he says, moving lower.

He nudges my thigh with his shoulder and I let my legs fall wide.

"Holy shit," I cry out at the swoop of his tongue. "Tyler."

My hands go into a panic, searching for something to grab onto. The sheets. The pillows. His hair. Any place that will help hold me down.

His tongue flicks faster; I feel his finger and then the second one working me until I can no longer catch my breath. I feel the spark building, and it's not taking its time.

"Oh my god." The sensation is going to overcome me any moment now. "Oh my god!" I scream, my body attempting to twist as Tyler holds me in place and somehow still manages to move his hand and mouth faster.

When I regain some type of composure, I glance down to see him grinning like a fool.

"That was fucking hot," he says.

My hand flies to my face and I mumble, "I can't believe you just did that."

"I'm going to do that more often," he says, climbing out of bed.

"Where are you going? Don't you want to … do more?" I ask.

Leaning his hands onto the bed, he says," More than you know, but we have a breakfast to get to, and then we need to get on the road."

"Hmm, food and driving over sex … are you sure you're the same guy I shared a bed with last night?"

"Ha ha. I sure as hell am, but I'm also the guy who promised his mom he'd show up for dinner when he got back, and I also told her you were coming," he says quickly, pushing off the bed and heading for the bathroom.

"You did what?" I yank the sheets up to cover myself. Talking about his mother makes me feel like I should definitely not be naked. "Tyler, I haven't seen your mom in years, and if I remember correctly, the last time I saw her was at the grocery store and I might have run from her."

"You ran from my mom?" he asks, pure entertainment on his face. "Like *ran*, ran?"

"I didn't *run,* run, I just walked away extra fast before she could see me."

"Well, if she never saw you——"

"Oh, she saw me. I was in such a hurry to avoid her that I knocked over a display of cereal boxes."

"What?" he asks, laughing. "That really happens?"

"Yes."

"Well, you shouldn't have done that. It's my mom. She'd have been thrilled to talk to you. She always asks about you," he says and disappears into the bathroom.

The shower starts, so I wrap myself in the sheet and take a seat on the toilet.

"Really?" I ask. How often did she ask about me?

"Yeah."

"What does she ask and what do you tell her?" My curiosity is getting the best of me.

"Well, up until a few weeks ago, I just said I see you around sometimes and that you're good."

"What? We hardly ever talked."

"What was I supposed to say?" he asks.

"Well," I start, but then I make the mistake of looking his direction. Holy shit. "Why don't you close the curtain?"

"Does it bother you?"

"It's kind of weird, yes."

"So then why don't you join me?"

I guess we're done talking about his mom.

I drop the sheet and join him. It's probably a good thing too. If we take separate showers and still have sex, we'll be more than just a little late for the breakfast.

* * *

"Morning," Sandy greets us as we join her and her husband at their table. The meet-and-greet breakfast is the last event on this weekend's agenda. I've really enjoyed the fact that Sandy and her husband have been our go-to couple here.

"Morning." I smile and take my seat as Tyler pulls it out for me. I immediately grab my menu. French toast or eggs Benedict?

Turns out, physical activity make you extra hungry.

"I'm almost sad to go home. If this is the kind of life I can live running the Colorado office, I'd be crazy not to do whatever I can to get the job," Sandy says with a smile.

Her eyes flash to Tyler. He's looking at the menu, and it appears that he didn't hear her, but I guarantee he did. He hasn't mentioned much about the type of competition he has for this promotion, so I'm not sure what to expect when someone else mentions it. Clearly, though, he's good at hiding what he's thinking.

"It would definitely be a great opportunity, and coming down here frequently to run things isn't a bad thing either. Especially in the summer," I say.

"Come down here frequently? You do know the job means …"

"Good morning, everyone," Mr. Jinks says into the microphone, hushing the chatter that has filled the restaurant and gaining Sandy's attention before she can finish her sentence.

"I want to thank each and every one of you for coming out here for the weekend. It's been wonderful, and I have no doubts that whoever receives this promotion will have no hesitation packing their bags and moving to this beautiful state."

Moving?

I'm not sure if Mr. Jinks keeps talking, because my attention is on Tyler. He never told me that getting this promotion would mean he has to move.

His gaze meets mine and, suddenly, I can't breathe.

"Excuse me," I whisper to the table and then quietly head for the doors.

I need air. I need it now.

Someone's chair screeches on the floor behind me, and I don't need to look back to see that Tyler is following me.

The cool air washes over my face as I inhale deeply. What was he planning to do? Just sleep with me till he moves? Why wouldn't he tell me this from the start?

"Abby."

"Are you moving to Colorado if you get this promotion?" I ask, spinning around to see his reaction.

His suddenly stiff form is all the answer I need.

"Wait," he says as I retreat down the steps toward the boat dock. Then his hand reaches for mine and pulls me back.

"Yes, the promotion comes with moving here," he says.

"You didn't think I needed to know that?"

"I didn't think it was necessary to share, no, not when it's not guaranteed that I'll get the job."

"Oh please, Tyler. Everyone in that room knows you're going to get it."

"People can think what they want, but until the day comes

that my boss actually announces my name, anything can happen. I didn't want to worry you. I didn't want you to think for one moment that my moving would affect us."

"But it will, Tyler."

I turn away from him focus on the lake. There's only one boat on the water now.

Tyler's hands cup my shoulders.

"I promise you it won't change a thing, Abby."

He kisses my left shoulder gently and then moves to the right.

My eyes drift closed. I want to believe him, but I've heard promises all my life and not a single person has kept one.

CHAPTER FIFTEEN

Tyler

See me in my office as soon as you get back from lunch.

Not exactly the note I wanted from my boss after a very delicious lunch with Abby. I'm not even mad that we didn't end up eating. That's been the norm since we've been back these past couple of weeks.

Colorado was beautiful, and I think Abby liked it just as much as I did. I bet she'd go with me if I asked her. I mean, we haven't exactly spent much time apart lately. Moving away from her would suck.

I knock on the frame of his door and wait for him to look up. His work phone is up to his ear; he waves me in.

He isn't smiling.

He always smiles when he sees me.

He also never emails me to come to his office as soon as I can.

This doesn't feel good. Something isn't right.

"Yes, thank you. I'll have more information for you later today. Yes. All right. Good-bye." Marshall sets the receiver down and sighs.

Oh no.

Did a client complain? Did the offer I made last week fall through?

He looks up, and I sit up straight.

Shit.

"Listen, Tyler. The reason I called you in here …" His voice is firm but wavers at the same time. Almost as if he isn't sure about what he wants to say. "My son, he's been making horrible choices for the past few years, and it's taken a toll on our family."

He pauses but keeps his focus on me. I want to cringe; this just got really weird really fast and I'm not sure what he wants me to do or say.

"Our family …" he goes on, this time rising from his desk to move around the room. I stay seated. "… has suffered in ways I can't even describe to you and in ways I'd never want you experience. The reputation it's given us, the countless therapy meetings and interventions we went through to get him to where he is today … it's not fun."

I imagine not. Why he is telling me all this?

"I don't like to share this depth of personal information with an employee, but because this certain … situation … applies to you, I decided this was best."

All right, wait. What?

"How exactly does this apply to me?" I ask, spinning my chair to face him as he stands near his bookshelf.

"You don't know?" he asks.

I shake my head. "I do not."

He sighs heavily and returns to his seat. He then begins to shake his head. "This is exactly how it started."

"I'm sorry, Mr. Jinks, but I need you to be more specific, because I'm pretty lost."

"Tyler, my son has relapsed and I'm afraid that the person who supplied him the drugs was your fiancée."

What the hell?

What is he talking about?

"That's not possible," I say.

"It's possible. My son hid this side of his life from everyone for a long time. I imagine your fiancée is doing the same."

"Abby doesn't sell drugs," I say without hesitation. "You have the wrong person."

"Tyler," Mr. Jinks starts, but I stand and cut him off.

"My fiancée isn't a drug dealer. Not now. Not ever."

"So you're saying my son lied to me?"

"Your drug addict son, yeah, I'm guessing he lied to you."

"That's out of line, Maron," Mr. Jinks says, and his voice makes me step back.

But I stand tall. "What's out of line is you placing the blame on the wrong person."

"I believe my son."

"I know my fiancée," I shoot back.

"Look, Tyler, I didn't ask you in here to argue about this. There is a truth to this story, and whether we know it or not, it doesn't change the fact that I can't have the Colorado branch run by someone who is linked to the distribution of illegal drugs."

Holy fuck.

"I'm not linked to the … this is bullshit. How can you say this to me without knowing the facts?"

"I can't risk it, and my guess is, neither my son nor your fiancée will confess the truth."

"She's not a drug dealer," I repeat.

Unless this is what Kurt was talking about when he referred to her on the phone that day at the golf course ….

Fuck. What am I even thinking?

It's not.

She wouldn't.

Screw this. I'm not sticking around to listen to him talk about Abby like this.

"Mr. Maron."

"What?" I snap, turning at the door to face him. "You want to tell me I'm selling drugs too? Or do you want to tell me someone else in my life is not who I think they are?"

"Why don't you take the rest of the day off, yeah?" he says. He even has the balls to say it like he's doing me a favor. "Let yourself take a moment and figure out what you want to do."

I open my mouth, the words *fuck you* fresh on my tongue, but instead, I force a smile.

"Yeah. I'll do that."

Getting out of here has never felt so good.

How could he say that about Abby? How could he even consider that Abby selling drugs is true? I mean … it's Abby. He's fucking lost his mind.

The doors to the building fly open as I step outside.

What in the actual fuck? Is this my life right now?

I slam my truck door and all but peel out of the parking lot.

I could hit someone. I could do more than just hit someone. I grip the steering wheel tighter and scream.

This is out of my hands, and not having control is about to make me lose control.

There's only one way to fix this.

I need to see Abby. If she knows something, anything, maybe I can figure this out.

What am I even saying?

Abby won't know anything. She not part of the drug world.

I'm just fucked.

Completely fucked.

Abby

I toss the last broken-down box from today's liquor shipment into the dumpster and head back inside. There are only five customers right now. I have one table and Logan has the other three people at the bar. Everyone seems content with their drinks, so I head over to Sara and Kelsey, chatting at a vacant table.

"Is that the new schedule?" I ask. Not that mine ever changes.

"No," Sara says. "Actually, it's an ad for the Silver Tap. I need to submit it to a few Colorado newspapers, and Kelsey is proofreading it for me."

"Ad for what?" I ask. "Did someone quit?"

The Silver Tap is The Black Alcove's sister bar in

Colorado. Sara opened it a few years back after her father bought it for her as a birthday gift, and it's had the same employees since the day they opened. I can't imagine someone leaving. It's the same as working here—the job is easy and the people you work for are laidback. Why would you quit?

"Not exactly. Liam's grandma is sick, and he wants to step down as manager to spend more time with her and help her out. No one wants to take his job, so it looks like I'll have to hire from outside."

"Oh."

If Tyler gets the promotion, I'd need a job, right? I don't have managing experience, but I know the business well enough.

"Can I apply?" I ask, and both Kelsey and Sara look up.

"Seriously?" Sara asks, and I pause a moment before I nod. She sincerely sounds relieved I asked.

"Yeah. I mean, I need to think more on it, but maybe."

"Yes. Of course you can apply. Just let me know." She digs in her bag and pulls out a sheet of paper. "It's not a proof-read copy, but it has everything you'd need to know about the job."

I skim over it quickly. I could definitely do this.

"Thanks," I tell her and head for the bar to find Logan.

Tyler will be so impressed. I can't wait to tell him and see what he thinks.

Wait.

Would my assumption that I'd move with him freak him out?

"Hey, Abby, how's your day?" Logan asks.

"It's fine. Yours?"

I'm waiting for his response when the door to the bar opens and a disheveled Tyler stands in the doorway. There's no smile on his face, and he looks like he hasn't slept in days.

"Excuse me," I say and meet Tyler at the door. I walk the whole way, too, because he hasn't moved.

Tyler steps back outside, and I hold my finger up to Logan. He nods, and I follow my boyfriend outside.

Boyfriend. Ha. So crazy, but so awesome.

Okay, stop smiling Tyler needs you to be serious.

"What's going on?" I ask and reach for him. He doesn't move, but he also doesn't return the affection.

"Did you ever think your whole life would be based off one decision?" he asks, and I lean back to look up at him.

"Isn't life all about the choices we make?" I ask. If he's starting the conversation out deep, then so will I.

"Yeah, but to know you worked so hard for something just to have it all taken away because of one person."

"You're going to have to be more specific because I don't think I'm following one hundred percent," I tell him.

"Mr. Jinks pulled me into his office today and basically told me that having you in my life will be the reason I lose this promotion."

"What!" I shout and take a couple steps back. "How? I mean, I …"

In one step he swoops me into his arms and presses his lips against mine.

"I'm not going to do it," he says. "I'd pick you over them any day of the week, Abs. Plus, his reasoning is total bullshit."

I'm almost afraid to ask.

"What was his reasoning?"

"That his son's drug relapse is because of you."

"What?" I say and my voice squeals.

"Exactly. He said you sold Kurt the drugs, and that he can't have the manager of the Colorado branch linked to the distribution of illegal substances."

"What the hell? That lying sack of shit! Kurt is the drug dealer, not me. If Mr. Jinks should be worried about anything, it's the fact that his son controls the drug market in most of this state!"

Tyler has stopped walking.

"What?" I ask, looking back.

"How would you know Kurt sells drugs?" he asks.

Shit.

"Oh, um. Most everyone knows that."

"No, they don't."

"Are you sure? Because maybe …"

"Because maybe you're not telling me something. Jesus," he groans, tugging at his hair as his breathing picks up. "Was he right? Are you connected to selling drugs?"

"No. Oh my god, no. Unless you count the fact that my mother used to be Kurt's delivery mule."

"What the hell, Abby!" Tyler shouts before he begins to pace.

"I'm sorry. I just didn't think it was important."

"Not important? You've known my boss's son this entire time and he knows you. You didn't think that, somewhere in the midst of all that has been going on, 'Oh, hey, Tyler might want to know this just in case he gets into a sticky situation?'"

"I didn't say anything, because who wants to admit their mother delivered drugs?"

"Am I not someone you trust?" he asks.

"Yes, you are, I just … I don't want to be the same girl you knew when we were kids. I didn't want you to still look at me like you felt sorry for me."

"Abby, that's not how I look at you."

"Really?" I ask. "Because a moment ago you were angry I didn't share this with you, and now that I have, you're looking at me like I could shatter any moment."

"I'm not," he says and reaches for my hand.

"You are," I argue.

"No. There is just a lot going on right now, and it's killing me that I have no control over how to fix it."

"Just go to your boss and tell him what I told you about my mother," I say.

"Really?"

"Yes, please. Anything to ensure I don't have to be around Kurt again." A shiver runs down my spine. "God, every time I saw him, I felt like I couldn't breathe."

"Yeah, I know."

"What?"

"I could tell you always got weird around him, but I just assumed it's because he's a creep."

"Let me get this right. You saw me uncomfortable and didn't bother to ask why or if I was okay?"

"Well …"

"Well, you had your chance to find out and never asked because you were too wrapped up in getting this promotion to care."

"Okay, hold up a second," he says. "We both could have handled this differently, but we didn't, and now this is where we are. So we need to move past it and figure out what to do next instead of fighting. That's not going to help anything. Agree?"

I fold my arms. He's right. "Agreed."

"Now, what I want to know is why Kurt would say it's you who is supplying him. I've met the guy less than a handful of times, and I know we didn't exactly get along—I mean, I caught him talking about you that day at the golf course, makes more sense now—but I didn't think I ever pissed him off so much that he'd go this far. I mean …"

Tyler's rant and recap of what he thinks happened is a great way to go about this, but I know exactly why Kurt did this.

"Tyler," I say, interrupting his theory that Kurt wants to run the Colorado office.

"What?"

"I know why he did this." I pause. The more things come out, the more my stomach aches, as if I'd been hiding something from him. Which, yes, but it's only because I was embarrassed.

"Well?"

"The short version is, that with my mom in rehab, he doesn't exactly have someone to do his dirty work. The weekend we were in Colorado, Kurt showed up and demanded I needed to fill her place since it was my fault she is in rehab in the first place. I told him no. He said I'd regret it. Now … this happens."

I swear, Tyler didn't even blink.

His head starts nodding and it keeps a steady bounce as he stares off behind me. "Okay then. That's that. End of story," he says and heads for the entrance of The Black Alcove. "Should we get a drink?"

What?

I quickly follow behind him.

"I'm still technically on my shift," I tell him. "But I think we should talk more about this."

"About me not getting this promotion or about how you've been keeping things from me when I was supposed to be someone you trust to share your worries with?"

Ouch.

"Tyler." I place my hand on his arm. "I truly didn't think this is what he meant by *regret*. If I had known he'd use it against you and this job, I'd have shared everything I knew with you in a heartbeat. Heck, I'll go find him right now and tell him I've changed my mind. Maybe that will get him to take back what he said and—"

"No, I don't want you to do that." Tyler kisses my forehead. "Just promise you won't keep anything else from me, okay?"

"Deal, but then you should know that I only agreed to be your fake girlfriend because I can't afford to pay for my mom's rehab, a place of my own, and also that freshman year of college. I was the one who Saran Wrapped your truck and then egged it. I also watched you struggle to clean it the next morning. Oh, and I also hate that you don't cook garlic bread with your spaghetti. You should always cook garlic bread with spaghetti."

Lame examples, I know, but the smile on Tyler's face is the first one he's cracked since he walked through that door.

With a quick peck on his cheek, I get back to work. I sneak a few glances at him over the next few hours, and even though he's acting like he doesn't care that his boss accused me of being a drug dealer or that he wants Tyler to choose between work and me, he does.

He's worked hard for that promotion, and I'm the reason there's a chance he won't get it.

Who wants to keep a girl around who puts a roadblock in their success?

No one.

CHAPTER SIXTEEN

Abby

Tyler hasn't been to work in three days.

I set the bowl of popcorn in front of us and then take the seat next to him. His phone is in one hand while the other wraps around me on the back of the couch.

"Do you want to watch *Step Brothers* or *Wedding Crashers*?" I ask, signing into his Amazon Prime account. I know they are two of his favorite movies, and I'm thinking that right about now, he could use some humor.

"I don't care," he says, his focus on his phone.

At least he heard me.

I glance to the clock.

"You know, if we changed right now, we could still make it for the last hour or so of the new employee meet and greet," I say.

"Nah, it's cool," he replies. His attention still on his phone.

Nah.

I freaking hate that word.

Nah.

Nah.

It just rubs me the wrong way. Something about the way the word lingers is like, it's an evil and sarcastic no. The kind you say when you're about to follow it up with something rude because you didn't like the original statement.

Or maybe I'm just overthinking all this. Maybe Tyler really doesn't want to be around his coworkers.

"Damnit," he shouts, causing me to jump, and then he rises from the couch. He grips his hair and heads toward the bathroom.

I wait for the latch of the door to click before I grab his phone off the coffee table.

A picture of Carl and Mr. Jinks on the company Facebook page pops up, and the caption reads: Our team turns friends into family.

Yikes.

I set his phone back down and slowly make my way to the bathroom. I knock once and wait.

"I'm fine, Abby. Just give me a minute."

"Oh …" I know Tyler, and he is anything but fine right now. "No, you're not."

I've just barely crossed my arms before the door swings open.

"You don't know how I feel," he snaps.

I swallow but don't move. "I have a fairly good idea."

"Abby, just stop," he says and walks away.

I'm right behind him.

"Look, Tyler, if you're not going because of me, that's stupid. You can go, and I'll stay here. It's not a big deal."

"It's a huge deal, Abby!"

This time, I jump at the boom in his voice.

"Marshall basically told me that as long as I'm with you, I don't stand a chance. What's the point if that's the case?"

"Um, because that's a stupid reason to not give someone the promotion. If you just give up, he'll think he was right about all of this, and he isn't."

"It's not that easy."

"It really is."

"Damn it, Abby, why won't you let this go?"

"Because you're clearly upset, and I want to try to make this better."

Taking a step toward me, he pulls me into him arms. "I'll find a way. You don't need to worry, all right?"

"I don't —"

"All right?"

He can tell me not to worry as much as he wants, but the truth is, I'm the reason he has to find a different way to get this promotion.

Did you ever think your whole life would be based off one decision?

His question from a couple of days ago smacks me like a ton of bricks. I never thought so, no. But what if I'm wrong and one mistake is all it takes to tear up the happiness I've waited my whole life for?

Tyler

I have the perfect idea.

It's brilliant. I can't believe I never thought of it sooner.

I swing open the door at the BA and immediately scan the

room for Abby. She's going to be so thrilled. Finally. Finally, we'll both get what we want.

She looks up from her table and smiles only momentarily before I've pulled her into my arms to kiss her. "I've got an idea."

"Really?" she beams. "Give me one second."

She turns back to her table and says something, but I'm too amped up to pay attention.

"Okay," she says and pulls me into the employees-only room. "Spill."

"I need to fake break up with you," I say, rushing out the words before I change my mind. "Tomorrow, you come into my work and we can get into an argument in front of everyone and then we can fake a breakup. Mr. Jinks will think we're over and I'll be back in the running."

It's a solid plan, but the Abby's squint hints that she might disagree.

"Fake breakup," she repeats.

"Yes."

"What happens after that? We sneak around and then you get the promotion and you hide me every time I go down there?"

"Just until he sees how great I am for the position and that nothing can get in my way."

Her eyes widen and she gives me a straight-mouthed smile. "That sounds like so much fun."

"Come on, Abby, I need your help."

"I think there are other ways to go about this, Tyler."

"How? Mr. Jinks doesn't believe a word I say to him."

"Still, I'm not sure I can stage a breakup with you," she says.

"It'll be easy. We'll chat like we're about to leave for lunch, then we can start arguing and—"

"Arguing about what?" she asks.

"You selling drugs," I tell her. "I'll make some comment about how you need to quit so we can move forward in our lives."

"Hold up. You want to stage a breakup where I admit I'm a drug dealer in front of your boss?" she asks.

"Yes."

How is she not understanding this?

"I'm not a drug dealer, and I'm going not to pretend that I am one." She shakes her head and moves toward the bar.

"Fine. Don't be a drug dealer. But I want this promotion, and I don't see any other way to get it. I need you to help me. I need you to help make this happen. I won't get it otherwise and then what? What do I do after that?"

Abby's chest rises, slowly dropping as she stares at me.

"This promotion. It means that much to you?"

"Yes."

"More than anything else?"

"Yes," I answer again and sigh with relief. She's finally getting it.

With a slow nod she says, "Okay, I'll see you tomorrow before lunch."

"Yes, oh my god, yes, thank you so much."

I kiss her on the forehead and head back to work. By putting myself back in the running, I've got houses to sell.

Finally. It's all falling together and in just a few weeks, I'll have it all.

CHAPTER SEVENTEEN

Abby

I once heard someone say, or maybe I read it somewhere, that people do really, *really* stupid things when they are in love.

I used to think it was bullshit. That love doesn't change people or make them act like a crazy person. Then I fell in love.

As soon as Tyler left the bar yesterday, I knew it was over. I can't keep letting him hurt me to get what he wants. I'm not an angel by any means, but I sure as hell don't deserve to have someone to treat me like this. Tyler knows I'd do anything for him. Maybe always agreeing to lie so he could get what he wanted was my mistake, but at some point, I thought he'd figure out that you don't take advantage of the ones you love. The moment you do, everything falls apart.

He wants me to fake a breakup—so what. But hiding me? Hiding us? That hurt, and I can't be with someone who's okay with that.

The elevator opens to Tyler's floor. Everyone is dressed professionally, focused on computers, cell phones, or tablets, busy with a full day's work.

Tyler is by a water cooler, standing next to Mr. Jinks.

I march straight for them.

Tyler starts to smile and then hides it poorly as he gets into his role. The look of pure disappointment on Mr. Jinks's face, however, isn't mistakable.

"I'll give you two some privacy," he says.

"That won't be necessary," I say and face Tyler. "It's over."

I pull the fake ring off and place it in his hand.

"What?" he asks.

I told myself I wasn't going to look up at him because I knew he'd be surprised. His plan was to dump me.

"We can't do this anymore."

"Abby, let's—"

"No, Tyler. The life you want and the life I want are completely opposite, and we just can't keep pretending we're happy." The last word falls off my lips right before he touches my chin and forces me to look at him.

"Abby." He sucks in a breath.

I know he sees it. I know he can see in my eyes that I'm not faking this.

Before he can reply, I head back to the elevator.

"Abby, stop," Tyler says behind me. My eyes dart around till I see the sign, quickening my steps to the stairs.

"Abby!" his shout echoes in the stairwell.

I know damn well that if I stood there for even a second longer, I would have crumbled under his gaze. He'd have said he was sorry, that mistakes happen, and I'd forgive him and we'd give this a go again. Till he needed me to fake something else for his gain, anyway. I don't want fake. I want real. One hundred percent real.

"Abby!" Tyler shouts again as he exits the building behind me.

"Abby!"

Ugh.

"What?" I snap, turning to face him.

"What the hell was that?" he asks.

"Us breaking up," I say, smoothing away the tears under my eyes.

"Yeah, but you don't have to keep crying. No one is watching us now."

"You don't get it, do you?" I ask.

"Get what? You didn't go to plan, but I still think that went okay. Don't you?"

"Tyler," I say softly and my heart pinches. I start to shake my head because I don't know how to say this to make him to understand.

"Meet you back at my place tonight for dinner?" he asks.

"No," I say,

"Your place?" His voice is shaky.

"I'm breaking up with you … for real."

Gosh, I sound like an idiot. We'd only been … whatever this was for less than a month. But with our history, it feels longer.

Our story is like your favorite song on repeat. It's the best thing you'll ever know, but eventually that love fades, and you still have to endure that song on a random day when you turn on your radio or step into a bar and hear it through the speakers.

I won't forget Tyler, but this, us, it can't happen.

"Abby, look. I—"

"No, you look. I've spent most of my life trying to be the right person for everyone around me. You were supposed to be the one I didn't have to pretend with. The one who wanted me for exactly who I am and not who they wanted me to be. Turns out I was wrong. I was wrong for so many years. I can't believe it took finally seeing what a life with you could be like to understand that you'll never want me for who I am."

"Abs—"

"Don't! Don't call me that. You don't get to use nick-names with me. You don't get to be cute. You don't get anything with me anymore."

His lip drops as if he wants to say something, but nothing comes out.

I turn for my car now, thankful he doesn't follow me.

I have no idea what comes next in my life, but what I do know is that I come first.

Tyler

"Hey, you've reached Abby. I'm clearly busy, so leave me a message and I'll probably text you after I get it."

I hang up when her voicemail comes through for what feels like the hundredth time in the last two days.

Why the hell won't she answer?

I know she's not in any kind of trouble, because when I saw Beth the other day, she told me Abby had been at work. So that means it's me.

I hop in my truck and drive toward the BA. It's a risky move, considering Kelsey, now my ex, works there, but if Abby won't answer my calls, maybe she'll talk to me in person. When I walk through that door, she won't really have a choice.

The after-dinner rush still fills the bar fairly well. I survey the room but don't see Abby.

What are the chances that I showed up on her night off? With my luck, that's exactly what's happened.

Logan nods from behind the bar, and I wave in reply then head for the bathrooms. Maybe Abby's back there. I just want to thank her and tell her my plan worked. Having her as a best friend is really the shit and I owe her one.

My fist is curled, ready to knock on the woman's door, but the voices on the other side stop me.

"What was he thinking?" a voice mixed with choked sobs asks. There is no mistaking it's Kelsey. "Abby was supposed to be my best friend."

"I know," another voice says. Beth. "Boys are dumb, and Abby is ... well ... I'm just as shocked as you are."

"How did this happen?" Kelsey asks.

"People do stupid things when they're drunk, babe. It happens."

"It doesn't happen to me," Kelsey cries. "I lost my boyfriend and one of my best friends all in one day."

What the hell? She didn't lose Abby, she just—

"You lost two people you don't need in your life. Abby lost everyone. Karma is a bitch and she's getting hers."

Whoa. Whoa.

"I can't ask you and Sara to stop being friends with her," Kelsey says, and I let out a breath.

"You don't have to. Friends don't do that to each other."

"Yeah, but ... "

"No buts, Kelsey. Abby fucked up. No one is going to see or take her side of this," Beth says.

"I should have seen this coming. I can't believe I didn't end things sooner."

"There is no excuse to use someone to get what you want just because of the friendship you have together."

I slouch against the wall and drop my chin as I keep listening. I shouldn't. I really shouldn't, but now I know why Abby won't call me back.

My shoulder droops as I look to my feet. I swear, that memory just stuck a needle into my heart.

I should have told them the truth right then. I should have done something, anything. But I didn't. I just let them think the worst of Abby because I was so damn worried that the truth would make things harder for me.

Fuck. I'm such an asshole.

What am I doing with my life?

I've asked myself this same question at least twenty times since Abby left me standing in the parking lot outside my office.

I have a good life. Good parents. A good job. Good friends. Good … everything. I don't have anything to be ungrateful for and yet, I needed more. That doesn't sound right. That sounds like someone greedy.

That sounds like me.

Thinking I could use Abby to get something more was an idiot move. Why is it that when people mess up, they only realize it after the fact?

Damn it. When have I ever done something for her? How have I ever helped her out? The answer is easy.

Never.

I shake my head and grab my keys off my desk. I don't know why I'm still here. I'm not getting any work done.

I take the stairs instead of the elevator and head for my truck.

Seven years ago, I fucked up. I was too scared to make things right because I didn't want to admit I did something wrong.

Well, like hell if I'm going to let another seven years go by before I do what's right.

Abby deserves better than what I've given her. It's about damn time I started to show it.

CHAPTER EIGHTEEN

Abby

I can't believe it took me this long to finally get a hold of my life. Is that normal? To be twenty-five and just figuring things out?

"You're really doing this?" Mason asks, and I nod.

"Yes."

It's hard not to miss the way he starts to smile but stops.

I know. It's both a sad and happy moment.

I sign my name at the bottom and hand him the clipboard. "That should be it."

"Yes, it is," he says. "Maybe we'll see you around sometime."

"Not here, I hope," I say, and this gets a laugh out of him.

"Agreed."

With a confident smile, I retreat down the hall.

This time, though, I'm not worried about how she'll treat me. I came here for a reason.

"Knock, knock," I say and step up to the bed. "I'm early today, I know, but I have news."

Her silence follows my comment as usual, but this time, it's different. The urge to cry isn't here anymore.

"Well, Mom, I guess it's time I tell you that I'm not coming back to see you." Even these words don't register a reaction with her. "I'll keep paying the bill, but if you don't want to be here, just check yourself out. I've completed all the paperwork for you to leave whenever you want. When you do, I hope you find what you're looking for and truly do hope you'll be okay."

I move for the door and still, nothing.

As I take my last steps down the hallway that used to hold so much hope, I finally feel like I can breathe. I may never have gotten the outcome I wanted, but I see now that it's okay. I wouldn't say I'm better off without her, but it's exhausting to love someone who will never love you. Also, I'm not sure I ever truly loved my mother. I thought I was supposed to because of our relationship, but then everything with Tyler happened, and I'm sick and tired of fighting.

I don't need anyone to love me but me. And I have that.

* * *

"Hey, Abby." Sara pokes her head out of her office. "Can we talk a moment in my office?"

"Sure," I say and close the door behind me. "What's up?"

"I know it's only been a few days since you mentioned wanting to manage The Silver Tap and I said I'd give you time to consider it, but I want you to know that if you want it, it's yours."

Wow.

"Are you serious?" I ask. This is unreal.

"One hundred percent. I honestly never knew you were interested in a management position."

"I didn't either, but then you mentioned it, and with Tyler possibly moving … you know what? It doesn't matter why. I didn't realize how much I'd enjoy it till I asked about it."

I need something different and with nothing to hold me in Wyoming anymore, why wouldn't I take the job?

"I'll take it," I say.

"Great!" she says and steps around her desk to hug me. "This is going to be so awesome."

I nod as my heart races. No turning back now.

"All right, I'll get all the paperwork ready. We'll need to discuss a start date and obviously find a place for you stay until you find a permanent residence. I know this sounds fast, but do you think you'll be able to be there by next week?"

"Next week?" I barely breathe out.

"Yes, I know. I'm rushing it, but technically I'm running both places from here, and it's taking every ounce of energy I have."

"Now I know why you offered me the job so quickly," I say and laugh.

"I'm desperate, yes, but I wouldn't have asked you if I didn't know you could handle it. Abby, you're a great employee and people love you. You don't take shit and you get things done. In a nutshell, that's exactly what I need."

"Great employee, shitty friend. Got it," I say.

Sara laughs. "I think Beth's candor is rubbing off on you."

"Maybe. I mean, I'd be okay with that. And if I'm on a

roll, I'm, uh, I'm sorry for not being the best kind of friend over the last, like, six or seven years."

"We've all had rough times. I wouldn't beat yourself up too much on it."

"Still, I should have been a better friend."

"Well, it's never too late to be that person again."

"Really?"

"Really. We all make mistakes, Abby. If you recognize your mistakes and learn from them, you're already a better person."

"I guess I should start by thanking you for this job. I won't let you down."

"I know you won't," she says.

I close Sara's door when I leave to check on my tables, and I can't help but wonder, if I had made the right choices … where would I be now? Would I have this newfound confidence, or would I still be pining for Tyler and praying my mom would change?

Doesn't matter.

I'm going the right direction now. I might be doing it alone, but sometimes, that's the best way to start.

Tyler

The street lamps pop on as I rest back against Abby's door. It's been two days since she broke things off with me. Two days that she hasn't answered my calls and two days I've talked myself out of showing up here so that she can have some space.

Now, it's been two hours and she hasn't come home yet.

I know she isn't working, because I went to the BA before

I came here. Luke told me she took the night off, so I assumed that she'd be here.

Maybe it's a good thing she isn't. I don't even know what I'm going to say. Sorry, obviously, but she deserves more than that one word. She deserves a reason why and I don't have one. I've been selfish. That's all I can chalk it up to. There was no reason for me to do what I did and yet, I still did it.

Headlights glow from around the corner, and Abby's car slows to a stop in front of the rental. With the engine still running, she watches me from inside the car.

Please don't drive away.

As if she heard me, the car shuts off.

"What are you doing here?" she asks softly. Like it took every ounce of her energy to ask the single question.

"I'm sorry, Abby."

"Tyler," she says with a sigh. "It's too late."

"It's not too late. I screwed up, I know that. I want to fix this. Nothing feels right when you're not with me. I need you more than I ever I knew did."

"No, you wanted your promotion."

"And you."

"Do you even hear what you're saying? I want to be someone's first choice, Tyler. I may not be a saint, but I deserve to be number one. Don't you think?"

"You are!"

"No. You would rather fake a breakup and hide me than be honest. You can't keep using me to get what you want. I'm done."

"Done? Abby, we—"

"Good night, Tyler."

"Abby, please don't shut me out like this."

Her shoulders drop. "Tyler. I'm moving. I took the manager position at the Silver Tap. I leave in a few days."

"What?"

"Look, since the day I met you, I don't know, I thought we were always more than friends. I hoped we were more than friends, but we aren't. I'm not even sure I'd call it that."

"I wouldn't. We're definitely more than friends. I'm an idiot. I'm going to do idiot things, but we—"

"Tyler, please," she says and her voice cracks. Looking up, she begins to cry. "Just stop. I can't do this right now."

I swallow the lump in my throat and nod. I just want to make it better and all I keep doing is making it worse.

I may not be able to say the right things, but I can sure as hell do them.

I just need one more opportunity to get it right.

Come on, Abs, please, *please* give me the chance.

CHAPTER NINETEEN

Abby

I need a drink.

Badly.

Waiting for Tyler to leave was painful. He stood and stared at the door for a good twenty minutes. Each minute made me want this drink more.

I stroll into the BA and find Beth and Kelsey sitting at the bar.

"Hey," I say, glancing at the clock. Nine is a late night for them.

"Hey," they say in unison, twisting to face me.

"Since you're not working … do you want to join us?" Beth asks.

Not drinking alone? Heck yes.

"I'd love to," I say.

I wander behind the bar and pop the top on a Stella Artois cider and then find my seat next to Beth.

"So, how are things with Tyler?" she asks.

I freeze mid drink.

Why would she ask me that in front of Kelsey? And, crap, now I have to say the situation is horrible, and they get to see karma working firsthand.

"Um, they're not," I say. "How's Maverick … or Ethan?"

Kelsey points her beer at me. "You can talk about Tyler. We broke up years ago. And also, I'd like to hear what happened. Maybe I can help."

It really would be nice to get someone else's opinion.

I must be crazy.

"Things are complicated," I say, and Beth snorts. "To make a long story short, Tyler asked me to play his fake fiancée and I said yes, even though I've always had a crush on him. Then, turns out, it went from fake to real and then … I sort of kept some stuff from him and then it sort of blew up again, which led to Tyler asking me to fake a breakup because he really wanted this job, which then led to me actually breaking up with him."

Beth starts shaking her head with an "I told you so" stare and Kelsey's bottom lip just hangs open.

"He just asked you play fake fiancée out of nowhere?" she asks. "That's so crazy.I mean … why would he do that?"

I glance between her and Beth. "Well, I've kind lied for him before and it worked out well for him, so I'm guessing he was in a bind and I … was free to help."

"When did you lie for him before?" Kelsey asks.

"Yes, do tell. You've never mentioned this before," Beth adds.

"For a reason. I do stupid things and that was one of them."

"Out with it already," Kelsey says.

I take a long drink. "I didn't so much as lie as I never corrected everyone who thought we had sex. Till Colorado, we never had," I say, and I swear I just swallowed a handful of cotton balls.

"What?" Kelsey asks calmly compared to the "What!" Beth just shouted at me.

I nod. "I know. It wasn't true. Could have been, though, which is why it held up so easily."

"Why would he want to lie about that?" Beth asks.

"Because I told him the only way we were breaking up was if he slept with my best friend," Kelsey adds. "So, he said he did."

"What in the hell?" Beth asks.

"I was so infatuated with him that I just went with it," I confess. "I thought I'd get more out of it, but instead, I lost every single friend I had."

"I still can't believe he would ask you to pretend to be his fiancée." Beth sounds like she's ready to punch him in the throat. "Or that you would agree."

"I can," Kelsey cuts in. "I mean, not that you agreed, but the Tyler part. I knew from the day I met you that you and Tyler had something special. I just didn't know how special until it was too late. Yet somehow, we just kept dating."

I shake my head. "It doesn't matter now. Friends or more than friends, neither is going to happen."

"I wouldn't call it quits yet," Kelsey says. "It took you two all this time to figure this out. You can't just jump right into a committed relationship without the work. You'll get there."

"I don't think so."

"Abby, think about it. In the end, every choice he's made

has always led him back to you. Every. Single. One. And that counts for something. I think it counts for a lot, and I don't think he's going to let this be it for you two."

Beth twirls her beer bottle and makes a humming noise.

"What?" I ask. Beth has never been one to hold back a comment.

She lets out her signature sigh and says, "You know, I'm always against your making stupid decisions, because you do it more than anyone I know, and I know what I said and how I felt about this whole fake engagement thing when you told me about it, but … once I saw the two of you together, something changed for me. Fake dating Tyler might not have been stupid after all."

I nod slowly. "You're right."

Beth smiles proudly.

"I make a lot of stupid decisions, but that ends now. I'm moving to Colorado for this job. My past has been nothing but heartache. It's time to focus on my future."

"That's not what I—"

"Thanks for the company," I say and toss my now-empty beer into the trash. "And Kelsey?"

"Yeah."

"I'm sorry."

A smile touches her lips and her eyes glaze over as she nods.

"Kick ass in Colorado, okay?"

"Will do," I say and open the door.

I step out into the summer air and take a deep breath.

I'm going to be happy, and there is only one person who can make that happen.

Me.

* * *

I'm going to miss living rent-free.

All I'd thought about when I moved in here was how I was going to get Tyler the promotion. I never considered how it would affect me when it was all said and done. And that was before our hearts got in way over their heads.

On the plus side, I've got a bag full of Chinese food and everything I own is packed up and ready to go for tomorrow morning.

I pull my keys out of my purse and freeze.

A single rose is taped to the front of the door. No note or message of any kind. Just a rose.

I peel back the tape and flower and head inside.

My heart speeds up when I see the trail of rose petals leading to the bedroom.

My first thought is to follow them, but what if Tyler is still here? Am I ready to talk to him again? He's always been able to read my face like a book and right now would be no different.

Then again, I don't exactly want to leave without saying something to him. Anything. Even if I just say good-bye.

I let out a long sigh.

What is wrong with me? I insist it's over and now I don't want to leave without seeing him.

Slowly, I follow the trail.

The door is cracked, and I can easily see if there's something on the bed. Opening the door farther, I see the room is Tyler free.

My hands shake as I step inside. There's a vase of roses on each nightstand and on the dresser, that one with a card. A picture of Tyler and me from junior high is propped up against the dresser mirror.

My hands are still uneasy as they peel back the envelope and pull out the card.

The front is white with a red and pink heart in the center.

I flip the small card open and quickly close it when I see Tyler's chicken scratch handwriting filling the entire center.

I haven't even read the first word and tears are already starting to pool in my eyes.

Damn it.

Why does love have to make me so damn emotional?

I take a breath and release, opening the card once more.

Abby,

Do you remember the day we met? You couldn't get the code on your locker to work and I showed up to help you. I never told you this, but Logan's locker was above yours. We'd been wandering the halls that day. I begged him to switch lockers with me. When he finally agreed, you should have felt how sweaty my hands grew, hoping I got the combo right on the first try. Boy, would I have looked stupid if I gave you instructions and then couldn't open it.

Anyway, the point is, you've had my attention since the day we met, and I was a stubborn boy who thought telling you this would cost me a friendship. Then one day, we weren't friends anymore.

You've always been someone who would put everyone ahead of yourself, and I took advantage of that. What I asked of you, it was wrong. I can't take it back and I can't give you back all the years you missed with your girlfriends or even me, but I want to give you the future you deserve. I want to spend my days proving to you that you are it for me and you will always be it for me. I want to give you a life that puts you first. You deserve to be first, Abs, and so much more.

I'm ready to put you first.

Please give me one more chance. I won't let you down.

I love you.

Tyler

Holy shit.

Tears drop off my chin to my shirt as I take a breath.

Holy shit.

I love you.

He loves me.

Holy shit.

Tyler

She never called.

I run my hand though my hair as I look at my watch.

Come on, elevator. Move.

If it weren't for Beth's text this morning, I'd probably still be lying in my bed, thinking about how I lost the girl. Her text wasn't this giant speech to tell me what to do, but … well, let's just say I should have done something like this a long time ago.

I can't believe it took me this long to figure this out. Nothing matters, not without Abby.

I glance at Beth's message once more.

. . .

Beth: I'm meeting Abby at the coffee shop across from the BA at nine. Then she's headed to Colorado. Pull your head out of your ass. This is my only text to help you.

The door dings open and I head straight for my boss's office.

His head is down, reading something in front of him, when I rush through his door.

I slide the piece of paper, slightly wrinkled from my grip, in front of him and step back.

"What's this?" Mr. Jinks asks.

"My resignation," I say, stuffing my hands in my pockets. "I'd give the recommended two weeks, but I don't have any open sale or bids pending, so I figure now is as good a time as any."

Pinching the bridge between his eyes, Mr. Jinks sinks into his chair.

"Tyler, I didn't expect for you to leave the company because of our conversation last week."

"I'm not."

"Then what spurred this decision?"

"It's time to start thinking of someone else for once. My life isn't just about me anymore, and if I keep going on the path I've been taking, well, I'll end up alone. I don't want that."

"Look, Tyler, I … Kurt was arrested last night. I know Abby had nothing do with his choices. I feel terrible for what I said."

"Thank you for that, but it doesn't change anything."

"There isn't anything I can say to change your mind?" he asks.

"Nope."

Nodding, he says, "Well, call me if anything changes."

"Thank you," I tell him, but I won't be needing his number.

I just need Abby.

* * *

By the time I pull up to the coffee shop, Abby's car is parked out front.

From a quick glance, it doesn't look like she's moving to another state today.

I park a few spots down and let out a long breath as I head in her direction.

She's sitting in the window across from Beth, laughing. I stop. I'm no idiot. The moment she sees me, that happiness will be gone. I'll just have to wait till they're finished.

Coincidently, they choose this moment to get up and walk out the door.

"I really wish I could stay longer," Beth says and hugs her.

"It's okay. I need to get on the road anyway. I have to sign my new apartment lease when I get there, and the sooner I get that done, the sooner I can settle in," Abby says.

"Well, I'll be down next weekend, so I'll see you soon," Beth says. After one more hug, Beth starts in my direction.

"About damn time," she says when passes me. "And don't give up."

I nod but turn my focus to Abby, who's waiting by her car.

"Are you mad?" I ask, approaching her.

"No. Beth told me she texted you, and it's fine. I wanted to say good-bye anyway."

"What?" I ask. "You're really going to leave?"

"Yes. Tyler, I told you, this is too complicated."

"It doesn't have to be."

"Maybe." She shakes her head. "But right now, it is." She hugs me quickly and then unlocks her car. "I have to go."

Her door has just barely closed when I hop into the passenger seat.

"What are you doing?" she asks.

"I'm going to Colorado."

"What?"

"You heard me. If you're going to Colorado, I'm going to Colorado. It's pretty simple," I say and buckle my seatbelt.

"Tyler," she says, and I have to admit that the way she laughs a little as she says my name sends a flutter through my stomach. *There's still hope.* "You can't just jump in my car and go to Colorado."

"Yes, I can."

"But you have a house and a job and responsibilities and—"

"And none of those things matter if I don't have you."

For the first time since she broke up with me, she doesn't have a reply.

"Did you get my letter?" I ask.

She nods.

"Did you read it?"

Again, she nods.

"I meant every word." I grab her hand. "I'm sorry it took me so long to figure things out."

Her head starts to shake and then she begins to cry.

"Hey, look at me," I say and guide her chin to face me. "I'm in love with you, and I don't want to be anywhere you're not. I don't want us to waste another six or more years because we're scared of what we could lose. Look at everything we could gain, Abs. I want this. I want you. Only you."

"What about the promotion?" she asks.

"Well, I quit my job, so there isn't one."

"What?"

"Yeah," I say with a small laugh. "I quit. Anything that comes between me and you isn't worth it. Ever."

"Oh my gosh, what are you going to do?"

I settle back into my seat

"I'm moving to Colorado."

My heart pounds as I wait for her to argue once more, but she doesn't.

She twists in her seat and her hands fidget in her lap. "I … I …"

"Abs." I lean over the center to grab her hands and look into her eyes. "If you love me too, and if you even have the smallest ounce of hope that we can still do this, you don't have to say anything, okay? Just pull onto the road and head for the state line. I'm not changing my mind. I meant it when I said I love you."

She nods, returning to her position staring out the window.

"I'm not playing any more games," she says.

"Me either."

"I want the real thing."

"And I want to give you that."

"I want a love that can't be broken."

Without breaking eye contact, I lean onto the center console and cup the side of her face with my hand.

"Baby, you're never getting rid of the love I have for you."

She drags her teeth over bottom lip and nods. Then, she starts the car and pulls onto the road.

"Holy shit," she says, turning my way with the biggest smile ever.

Holy shit is right.

I just got the girl.

EPILOGUE

Six months later ...

Abby

Whoever said moving would be fun clearly never had to unpack a kitchen.

I twist, taking in the amount of counter and cabinet space around me, not to mention the island. The size of this single room is about half the size of my old apartment. Not only are the cabinets real oak, but the countertops are marble and the floors are hardwood and it's just ... it's the best thing ever.

"Hey, beautiful." Tyler saunters into the room, scooping me up as he wraps his arms around me. He kisses my neck, and when he pulls me against him, my body instantly warms at the skin-on-skin contact. I turn in his hold and come face to face with a shirtless Tyler.

"Have I ever told you how much I enjoy it when you don't

wear a shirt?" I ask, leaning forward to kiss his bare chest. He groans, gripping my hips and lifting me.

My shorts do nothing to help my butt from growing cold against the countertop. I squeal both from the sudden coldness and from the sight of Tyler as he spreads my legs to stand between them. He captures my lips with his own then bites on my lower lip as he pulls away.

"I also really enjoy it when you're not wearing a top," he says. His hands move to remove my T-shirt, but I stop him.

It's challenging to turn him down, especially when he starts kissing me from my lips to my cheek to my neck … and down.

"Tyler, you know I have to be at work early today if we want to get on the road in time to make it to Wind Valley for the Christmas party," I tell him and then push him away gently with my foot.

He folds forward with a groan, his hand never leaving my thighs.

"All I need is five minutes," he says.

"We all know what your five minutes means." I laugh.

"Okay, fine. Ten."

"You'd take twenty," I say and kiss him. "And I'd want to give you my entire day."

"God, I love you," he says. He grabs my hand to help me off the counter then slaps my butt as I round the island to finish unpacking the plates.

He pulls up a seat across from me.

"You know, I thought this place was nice when I first looked at it, but with you standing here in in those cheeky shorts and T-shirt, I'm pretty damn sure this is the only place I'll ever want to be," Tyler says.

After all our time together, he can still make my cheeks turn beet red. Which I love.

I point at him with the plate in my hand.

"Your mouth is just as bad as your hands," I say.

He chuckles and then gets off his stool.

"Don't," I say and back up. "I'm serious. I have to finish unpacking this box and then get to work."

He pauses. "If you want me to stop, don't smile."

I stop smiling, but I can feel the twitch at the corner of my lips.

"I said don't."

"I'm not."

He makes a funny face and then starts to do a silly dance.

I have to press my lips together, and then I look away before he sees me crack.

"I know you smiled," he says, stepping over a box and pulling me into him once more as I laugh.

"You didn't play fair," I say, and it's all I get out before he kisses me. This time I don't stop him.

Five minutes behind schedule won't kill me.

* * *

"Holy balls, it's cold here," Tyler says, pulling me into his body as we make our way from the parking lot to the BA.

"Too cold," I agree as my teeth chatter.

A gust of warm air engulfs us the moment we step inside. "Jingle Bells" is playing from the jukebox as my coworkers and friends fill the room. Kids are running around playing with toys and —

"Oh my god," I say and fold over with laughter.

"Is that Logan?" Tyler asks.

I nod repeatedly as we both stare at our friend.

"I mean, at least when he gets old and the white beard is for real, he can rock it," I say.

"You made it!" Beth greets us as she rises from her spot at "the" table and hugs us both.

"We weren't sure if you made it through before they closed the roads."

"Barely," Tyler says. "But there was no way we were missing this."

"Good," Beth says quickly, giving Tyler a strange look.

"I need to use the bathroom. I'll be right back," Tyler says and kisses my forehead before stepping away.

"So, things are good?" Beth asks.

"Too good," I say. "I swear, he has been so perfect, and I still can't believe that this is my life."

"I'm happy to hear that," she says with another hug.

"Abby," Kelsey calls out, leaning back in her chair. "Do you want to join us?"

Did she …?

I glance between her and Beth and then notice Sara sitting at the table watching me, also waiting for my answer.

She totally did!

"Yes," I say once I've found my voice. "I'd love to."

I've only made it one step before I notice all three of my friends focusing on something behind me.

I twist and stumble back, my hand covering my heart as I take in the scene before me—the man I love is down on one knee. My name isn't even off his lips before I'm on my knees, too, and kissing him.

It's a kiss I'll never forget. It screams love and passion.

He chuckles and breaks it off. In a whisper, he says, "You know I'd like more than anything to keep that going, but people are watching, and I came here with a purpose."

I laugh and nod, dropping back on my heels and wiping away the last of the tears.

"Do you want to stand?" he asks, and his hands shake as he grabs mine.

"No," I say and never let my eyes break from his.

He blows out a breath. "Abby James …" he begins, and I'm already starting to cry again. My heart is pounding hard.

"You are the most amazing woman I've ever met, and ever since the day I saw you struggling to open your locker, I knew I'd always want to be here for you."

I let out a small laugh and so do a couple others. "I can't imagine my life without your beauty, your strength, your passion, and your love. That's all I need. Just one love. Ours. For the rest of my life. Will you please do me the honor of being my wife?"

The black velvet box in his hands opens to reveal the most elegant, round, yellow diamond I have ever seen.

My eyes widen, and I nod. I nod so damn hard I could break my neck.

His arms snake around my back and he embraces me tightly. He holds me like his life depends on it. I know this because that's exactly how I'm holding him, and I don't plan on letting go.

***

Want exclusive content delivered right to your inbox?

Subscribe to her mailing list for exclusive bonus epilogues
and all the book news!

Ready for more by Jami Rogers?
Check out, Kiss Me Crazy, a steamy enemies to
lovers/roommates romance by Jami Rogers today!

KISS ME CRAZY
CHAPTER ONE

Lennox

Find a partner.

The three worst words to hear when you're either the new kid in gym class where you don't have any friends or when it's the first day of sophomore year college courses and you don't know a single person in the room.

I glance around, watching people pair up two by two. The chances of someone choosing me as their partner decrease by the second.

I adjust myself in my seat, crossing one leg over the other and fold my notebook back, ready to take notes.

I don't need a partner anyway. I'm better off on my own, a sure bet my assignment will be on time. Explaining to someone why the assignment would have to work on my schedule sounds like such a pain in my ass. Let's hope Professor Turner, who's also been my advisor since I began classes here last year, sees it that way, too.

"Does everyone have a partner?" he asks, projecting his voice in a way that makes everyone look around the room to confirm instead of someone actually just saying yes.

His gaze lands on me, narrows, and then his short, black-haired head tilts to the right as he sighs. Professor Turner has this whole current-day John Cusack thing going on. It fits him.

"Lennox, where is your partner?" he asks. The fact I enjoy working alone won't be lost on him. I've expressed my need to not rely on others more than a time or two in his office. I'm certain he's sick of hearing me tell him I don't need help picking out my classes, but he still insists we meet a few times a semester.

I smile but keep my focus on the blank college-ruled paper on my desk. No doubt, the entire class is looking at me. I pinch my lips together before I look up.

"You know, I was thinking I could handle all the projects solo this semester, Mr. Turner."

He shakes his head. "That's not how this course is planned." I laugh a little.

"I'm basically telling you that I'll gladly do double the work, and you're telling me no?"

He sighs heavily, like before, tapping his finger on the corner of his desk. His mouth opens to say something, but he's interrupted by the classroom door swinging open and slamming against the doorstop. A *zing!* rings throughout the class.

Oh, my hell.

Tripp McCain.

Please tell me he's only here to drop something off. My

blood has already started to boil and I'm just looking at him. No one can ruin my day more than the jackass standing in the doorway, wearing his perfect tailored jeans and perfect collared shirt that probably cost more than my cell phone bill the last three months combined.

Please. Please. Don't stay.

I turn back around in my seat. If I don't make eye contact, maybe he won't see me and I can relax.

"Can I help you?" Professor Turner asks.

"Is this Creative Writing 1020?"

"Yes. It is. Class started ten minutes ago."

"I got lost."

Liar. He's been going here longer than I have. I can't help but roll my eyes.

"Well, come on in. Class already started and your partner is waiting on you." *No!*

"Sweet. Who's my partner?" he asks. "Lennox Ashby."

"No," I say rather louder than I'd planned.

"What?" Tripp says at the same time. I twist to glare up at him only to find him scowling down at me.

"Anyone want to trade partners?" he asks the class. A few of the guys chuckle, and one girl raises her hand immediately behind him.

"Oh please, you don't get to be the one annoyed by this," I say.

"And yet somehow I still am."

"Enough. No one is trading partners. Take a seat next to Ms. Ashby. This isn't high school anymore," Turner instructs, turning to write something on the whiteboard behind him.

"I'd rather withdraw from this class than endure any

amount of time with you," I whisper once he's seated. His wintergreen scent carries through the air, reminding me of Altoids. Screw his perfect smell, too.

"Wow, I think that's the first thing we have ever agreed on."

We turn at the same time, both glowering at each other. His dark blue eyes are bright against his light skin and black hair.

Ugh. What is it about attractive guys always being jerks?

There once was a time when I thought Tripp was this amazing, kind person, and my heart would speed up whenever he was around me.

I throw up a little in my mouth—not really, but the memory

that at one point in our lives I truly thought he was a good person damn near makes me—and look away. That was three years ago.

There are a lot of shitty people in this world, but the number one person among the shitty people I actually know is sitting right next me.

"If you don't already know your partner, introduce yourself and exchange contact information if needed. This person is now your lifeline for my class. If you are going to be late, absent, or anything else comes up, this is the person to contact. They will relay the information to me and bring you any missed assignments. Working with your partner will account for twenty percent of your overall grade." I groan and so does Tripp.

Hey, he has nothing to back up his attitude. Me? I have a whole freaking novel of reasons.

The worst part? I need this class if I'm going to get into the summer journalist program. I can't afford to pay for a spot out of my own pocket. I need to pass this class if I want any chance at a scholarship for next year, too. Which means I don't have a choice of whether I work with him or not. Perhaps I should have taken this class last semester like Turner suggested after all.

"Drop the class," Tripp leans over to whisper.

"You drop the class," I whisper back.

"Come on, Lennox. Drop it."

I don't say anything back to him or anything else at all for the remainder of class. The moment we're dismissed, I shove everything in my bag and hightail it out of the room. The less time with Tripp the better.

"Lennox!" Kass, my best friend, shouts over the other students shuffling through the hall. "We're going to go get lunch. Do you want to come?" she asks.

"Who is we?" If she's going to lunch with her boyfriend and he invites—

"Let's see." Kass forces a smile when Tripp begins to answer for her. "It'll be you, Kass, Mark, Winston, and myself," he says.

"Lovely," I say, laying the sarcasm on thick.

At least Tripp didn't include his girlfriend in that list. I dislike her probably more than him. Put the two of them together and, well, hanging around them is like eating black licorice and wasabi at the same time. Absolutely the last thing I would ever choose to do.

I thought the worst part about today was being forced to be partners with Tripp for class, but it's not. It's being reminded that he is one of my best friend's boyfriend's friends.

"I honestly don't know why you keep asking Kass who "we" is when she invites you to do something. The answer is always the same," Tripp says.

"Wishful thinking on my part," I say and adjust my bag over my shoulder.

"Think you two will ever get along?" Kass asks.

"No."

"No."

Like many times before, I give Tripp a look that, in my mind, sends him running through campus with his hair on fire.

"I have some things to do at home before classes this afternoon and work tonight. Rain check?" I ask Kass. Even though I can get a lot of homework done at the tanning salon, where I work, I still try to do most of it at home before I go. So my excuse isn't a lie to get out of spending more time around Tripp.

Convenient, but not a lie.

"Oh, don't miss on my account," Tripp says.

"Your presence doesn't affect me," I say.

This time it's Kass who rolls her eyes. "Okay, I'll text you later."

I wave goodbye and head back to my apartment located three blocks from campus. Despite Tripp, I'd love nothing more than to enjoy a carefree lunch with my friends, but my wallet just won't let me do that. My budget allows me just enough to get by. Kass, Mark, Winston, and Tripp especially will never know what it's like to struggle financially, and if I have anything to say about it, they will never know that I do.

Tripp *Fine.*

One word that almost never actually means what it means when a woman says it, but right now, I don't give a shit.

I tap the red circle on my phone to end the call and walk back inside the restaurant, sliding into the booth next to Winston.

"Was that Sydney?" Kass asks.

I nod.

"Why don't you just break up with her?" Winston asks.

I shrug. I've considered it many times. Our relationship is all kinds of weird. To sum it up, I have money, which she likes, and she does anything I want, whenever I want, which is less drama for me. We're used to our arrangement, and there aren't any actual feelings involved. Well, on my side, there aren't and as for Sydney, as long as I am paying, she'll agree to anything if I ask her to. No surprises. Just the way I like it. It works for us.

"She's not so bad most of the time," I say. Today isn't that day. She's pissed off that I didn't want to take her to the country club across town for lunch, which resulted in her staying on campus to eat. I told her I'd call her later, and all she said was "fine." That was the end of the call.

None of my friends like Sydney, and Lennox especially hates her. Maybe that's part of the reason I keep her around. Then again, pissing off Lennox isn't hard to do.

"They just gave you a Range Rover?" Mark asks, his gaze out the window.

I shrug. I knew offering to drive everyone to lunch would lead to questions, but I really wanted an excuse to take my new car for a spin. I was beginning to think my parents didn't really know me, but when a black 2019 Range Rover SVAutobiography Dynamic showed up on my doorstep with solid black leather interior, I wasn't going to complain. I probably should have called or messaged them to thank them, but it's been more than a week and they've yet to get in touch to see if I actually got it.

"Call it an early birthday gift," I say. Of all my friends, Mark should know better than to bring up any topic of conversation that leads to talking about my parents. I'll steer clear of it every time. Unless they are buying me something, they don't give a shit about me.

"Your birthday was last month," Kass says. The confusion on her face is normal. The fact that Mark's girlfriend has no clue is why I trust him more than I trust anyone.

"Whatever. I don't question them. My parents do whatever they want," I say, taking a bite of my burger. Plum's is the best burger place in town. Maybe even the whole state of Wyoming, and with as often as we come here, I'm going to need to double up my gym time sooner rather than later.

Mark and Winston chuckle while Kass focuses her attention me.

"I think I'm starting to see why Lennox doesn't care for you," she says. Her lips twitch to a smile.

"Oh really? Please explain it to me, because your parents have lived in the same townhouse right next to my parents for as long as I can remember, and I don't recall any moment when you questioned the clothes, jewelry, or limos to and from school that they gave you."

Kass laughs and tosses a fry at me.

"Yes, but I've grown up since then." "Have you though?" I joke with her.

"Yes, she has," Mark answers for her and kisses her temple.

Mark and Kass knew each other back in New York, before I moved to the neighborhood, and those two have been in a relationship longer than I can remember. We chose to go to school in Wyoming because we all wanted to leave the East Coast and get as far away from our parents as possible. They have chosen a path that cuts them off a bit more; I still let my parents give me anything they want. The thing my parents don't know is, it's going to take a lot more than buying me things to make up for being absent my entire childhood.

"Why didn't Lennox come?" Winston asks. Winston was also a reason we chose Wyoming. He used to go to school with us until his parents moved him here. So we've all known each other for almost ten years at least. Lennox became Winston's friend after he moved here, so obviously we all just hang out together despite the fact she and I can't stand each other.

I raise my hand, gaining everyone's attention, and then pop a fry in my mouth.

"I'm always the reason she doesn't come," I say between bites.

"Not true," Kass says. "Lennox just has different goals than us. She's very focused on her future."

Too focused if you ask me. Last semester, she ditched out on more parties than anyone I know so she could study. In fact, now that I think about it, I don't think she went to a single one. Serious people who can't even take a day to enjoy life drive me insane. They aren't people worth being around. I'm allowed to say that because I grew up with two people who are exactly like that.

"That's what people call boring," I add, keeping my opinion short.

"Oh, stop it, Tripp. You secretly like her. Admit it," Kass says.

"Yeah, I won't because I don't."

She has legs I could stare at all day, the perfect ass, and occasionally a smile that makes me forget how much I hate her. None of that means I secretly like her. It just means I can tolerate her enough to be around her when we are all together.

"She's nice to look at," I say, and Winston jokingly slugs me.

"Maybe if you took time to get to know her, you'd think differently," he says.

Winston is always defending Lennox.

"The day I admit I secretly like her is the day you admit you've been in love with her since you met her."

"I don't love her ... not like that anyway." He looks back to his phone, most likely texting Lennox. "You guys just don't know her like I do."

I don't miss the quick glance he and Kass share.

He's in love with Lennox. I'm sure of it.

"She didn't come. So what?" Mark says. "She does what she wants. If anyone knows how to do that, it's you, Tripp. Let's move on to a different topic. The frat party on Friday. Are we going?"

"Of course we are," I say. "We're only young once."

"Don't you have to do that thing for that program you're trying to get into this weekend?"

"That thing?" I raise my brow at Winston. He's probably referring to the paper I have to write for the summer journalism program I have my eye on. Along with successfully passing the assigned creative writing course, you have to write multiple papers throughout the semester and turn in each one by a certain date to be considered for the scholarship that pays for you to attend the journalism program. The first essay is due Monday. "I have all weekend to do *that thing,* and if I don't, I'll just pay for my spot. It's not a big deal."

Winston shakes his head.

I twist to my left to face him. "What? I can see you have more to say."

"I just don't understand why you're in college if you're not actually going to try."

"I try," I argue.

"You take two classes a semester. You don't try hard." He tosses a fry into his mouth.

"I pass the classes I take, so I think I do."

Winston holds my gaze for a moment and then smiles.

"Fuck, I wish I could just not care the way you don't," he says.

"It's called not choosing to be a doctor," I point out.

"Yes, but he'll be the best doctor," Kass says, smiling proudly at Winston.

"I wouldn't trust anyone else to deliver our babies when that time comes," Mark says.

"Exactly." She laughs and then stands. "Let's finish this damn week so we can go to that party already."

Our chairs scrap against the floor as we stand. Winston crumples his burger wrapper and shoots it into the trashcan. He misses. I pick up the makeshift ball and sink it right into the center of the bin.

I shove him as he rolls his eyes then make my way to the register to pay our bill.

"Better luck next time," I say as he leans back against the wall to wait for me.

"Sir, this card doesn't work," the brunette behind the counter almost whispers to me.

I shake my head.

"It does that sometimes. You can manually enter it," I tell her.

"Been using the plastic too much?" Winston asks. "I swear you use that thing more than my own mother. Shit, more

Amazon boxes appear on her doorstep than flies." I chuckle.

"I don't use it that much."

"Sir," the woman says again, "I'm really sorry, but it's not working."

"Fine," I say and hand her another card.

Her response doesn't change.

What the hell?

I reach for a third card, but Winston drops one onto the counter first.

"I got it."

I slap him on the shoulder. "It's about damn time you paid for a meal," I joke.

I tuck my wallet into my back pocket and make a mental reminder to call the bank.

There's no way all my cards stopped working.

Shit. It's probably because I used that sketchy ATM outside the movie theater the other night. Goddamn scammers are everywhere these days.

"Finally," Mark shouts as Winston and I step outside. "How about letting me take the wheel this time?" Mark points to where my car is parked.

"Whoever catches them first gets to drive," I say and toss my keys into the air.

Keep reading Kiss Me Crazy today!

Don't want to miss out on any new releases from Jami? Subscribe to her mailing list for exclusive bonus epilogues and all the book news!

MORE BOOKS BY JAMI ROGERS

The Black Alcove Series

Just One Kiss

Just One Night

Just One Touch

Just One Moment

Just One Spark

Just One Love

The Kiss Me Crazy Series

Kiss Me Crazy

Love is Crazy

I Want Crazy

The Evergreen Brothers Series

A Boyfriend by Christmas

The Summer Wedding Hoax

A Match by Christmas

The Lust or Bust Series

The Write One

Write About You

The Write Choice

Write That Down

More Than Write

Always Been Write

Standalone Novels

Love Money

Date in the Dark (A New Years Eve Novella)

ACKNOWLEDGMENTS

I am so incredibly thankful for all the people who helped make this book, and the entire series, a journey I'll never forget. That said, this book was the hardest book for me to write. I put it off. I avoided it. I didn't exactly want to write it. In fact, I'm writing this line and the book isn't even finished. I still have a good 15k in words to go. I'm still stalling, but now, I'm confident in the story, and I hope you enjoyed it.

Two people who have made the biggest impact on this story are Julie Sturgeon, my editor, and Dana Volney, a truly amazing friend and the best critique partner on earth. (Quick FYI—Dana introduced me to Julie.) Dana, you read all the crap versions of my stories and help me turn them into caterpillars, and Julie, you make them become butterflies. I know that sounds cheesy, but I don't care. You are both so important to me, and I can't wait to continue working together.

Mom, Dad, and Holly: Your continued support never goes unnoticed! I love you and miss you all.

A huge thank you to my far-away friend, Christian. You read my books and you constantly encourage me to keep going. Thank you for being a rock. Move to Wyoming. #SFL #Squad

Copyedits and Proofreading: Thank you, Casey Dawes,

for giving me that extra boost of confidence, knowing I've put my best work out there.

Grant, the husband with more patience than I'll ever know, thanks for sticking around and keeping me motivated! If I didn't have you to keep me in line, I'm not sure where I'd be right now.

InkSlingerPR: As always, you do an amazing job at organizing cover reveals, blog tours, release days, and more! Thank you for helping me spread the word.

Readers and bloggers: You make this happen. Without you, I wouldn't be where I am today. You believe in me and all of my books, and I can never thank you enough.

ABOUT THE AUTHOR

My name is Jami Rogers and I write new adult contemporary and adult contemporary romance novels. I *love* love and want to share my passion for happily ever afters with the world.

I was born in Wyoming and still live in the cowboy state with my husband, daughter, and two dogs. I like to read, write, run, watch movies/TV and spend time with my family. I'm horrible at returning phone calls and prefer to text, but still struggle to hit the little blue arrow to send a message once I'm finished typing my reply. My husband does 90% of the cooking in our house. Not because I'm busy – I'm just simply a bad cook.

Keep up with Jami by visiting her website www.
authorjamirogers.com
or
Subscribe to her mailing list for exclusive bonus epilogues
and all the book news!